BÉNÉDICTION

D'UN

ORATOIRE DE NOTRE - DAME - DE - LOURDES

A SAINT-FARON, PRÈS DE MEAUX

MEAUX

LE BLONDEL, IMPRIMEUR-LIBRAIRE DE L'ÉVÊCHÉ

RUE SAINT-REMY, 2, ET PLACE DE LA CATHÉDRALE

—

1886

BÉNÉDICTION

D'UN

ORATOIRE DE NOTRE-DAME-DE-LOURDES

A SAINT-FARON, PRÈS DE MEAUX

MEAUX

LE BLONDEL, IMPRIMEUR-LIBRAIRE DE L'ÉVÊCHÉ

RUE SAINT-REMY, 2, ET PLACE DE LA CATHÉDRALE

—

1886

BÉNÉDICTION

D'UN

ORATOIRE DE NOTRE-DAME DE LOURDES

A Saint-Faron, près Meaux.

Le jeudi 15 juillet 1886, la paroisse du Plessis-Placy, au canton de Lizy-sur-Ourcq, et toutes celles qui avoisinent le plateau élevé du Multien, étaient en fête : Mgr de Briey, évêque de Meaux, devait bénir un oratoire de Notre-Dame de Lourdes érigé dans le domaine dit de Saint-Faron. Cette propriété appartenait jadis à l'abbaye fondée dans sa ville épiscopale par le dix-neuvième évêque de Meaux ; elle a passé entre les mains de M. Foucher, chevalier de la légion d'honneur, notaire honoraire de Paris et ancien maire du IXe arrondissement.

Secondé par sa digne épouse, M. Foucher répand des bienfaits autour de lui, en même temps que ces chrétiens exemplaires prêchent par leurs actes l'obéissance aux préceptes de la religion. Pleins de confiance en la Mère de Dieu, les châtelains de Saint-Faron étaient à Lourdes à l'époque des deux pèlerinages meldois ; ils en sont

revenus avec le désir d'implanter en notre Brie
la dévotion à la Vierge des roches Massabielle.
Dès 1883, ils placèrent dans une tourelle de leur
habitation une statue de la madone de Lourdes ;
elle devint aussitôt un but de pèlerinage régional
qu'un visiteur baptisa du nom bien choisi de
petit Lourdes. Douze mille pèlerins sont déjà venus se prosterner devant elle : beaucoup y éprou-
vèrent consolation pour l'âme et même soulage-
ment pour le corps.

Afin de favoriser cet élan aussi spontané
qu'inattendu, les deux époux préparèrent à la
reine de la France une demeure plus digne d'elle.
Un oratoire lui fut ménagé dans le corps même
de leur résidence d'été ; la statue déjà célèbre fut
mise dans une niche reproduisant l'anfractuosité
où l'Immaculée apparut dix-huit fois à Bernadette. Avec la sainte hardiesse des enfants de
Dieu, les donateurs sollicitèrent de Mgr de Briey
pour ce gracieux sanctuaire une bénédiction solennelle. Le quatre-vingt-dix-septième succes-
seur de saint Faron y consentit d'autant plus
volontiers que c'était pour lui l'occasion d'hono-
rer tout à la fois et la sainte Vierge, patronne de
sa cathédrale avant saint Etienne, et l'un des
neuf saints qui se sont assis sur le siège épisco-
pal de Meaux.

† † †

Au jour fixé, Sa Grandeur arrivait accompa-
gnée de M. Moret, archidiacre du Gâtinais.

— 7 —

M. Perdrau, chanoine honoraire de Paris, curé
de Saint-Etienne-du-Mont, cousin de M. Foucher,
avait précédé le prélat. Plus de vingt prêtres se
trouvaient réunis autour de M. Hazard, curé du
Plessis-Placy depuis trente-sept ans ; mention-
nons MM. Bernard et Barbier, curés des deux
paroisses de Meaux ; M. Pichelin, chanoine honoraire ; M. Thiercelin, aumônier de l'hospice de
Meaux, organisateur si habile des pèlerinages
meldois ; M. Enguérand, doyen de Lizy, presque
tous les curés de son canton et plusieurs des
cantons circonvoisins. On remarquait avec atten-
drissement M. Vigne, curé de Crouy-sur-Ourcq,
dont la volonté maitrisait la souffrance.

L'assistance atteignait trois mille personnes
accourues de tous côtés, voire même de la ville
épiscopale. La municipalité du Plessis-Placy
témoignait par sa présence de son approbation
pour cette fête religieuse. Deux cents jeunes filles
au moins, dont plus de la moitié en vêtements
blancs, étaient groupées derrière les bannières
paroissiales. La première bannière, et de beaucoup la plus artistique, qui appartient à Mme Foucher, a figuré avec honneur à Lourdes aux pèlerinages diocésains de 1883 et 1885 : d'un côté
elle représente la Vierge de Lourdes, et de l'autre
saint Faron. Les plus jeunes enfants portaient
des oriflammes bleues comme la ceinture de la
céleste visiteuse de Bernadette. Ces bataillons
de vierges manœuvraient sous la direction des
dames Augustines, de Lizy, des filles de la Cha-

rité, de Varreddes, et des sœurs de la Présenta-
tion, de May. Un certain nombre de garçons
marchait aussi sous un étendard sacré.

La veille, le temps avait été des plus mauvais ;
ce jour-là, le soleil brillait comme un sourire de
la reine du ciel à ses enfants assemblés en son
honneur : pour faire mieux apprécier cette faveur, des nuages menaçants apparaissaient à
l'horizon. Au moment de la mise en marche, des
gouttes de pluie tombèrent sur la foule. « C'est
de l'eau bénite », s'écria une intrépide croyante
qui avait compris le beau temps dans son pro-
gramme.

A onze heures précises, la fonction commence
par une procession à travers le petit parc. Sur le
seuil de l'oratoire, M. le curé du Plessis-Placy
remercie son évêque en ces termes :

Monseigneur,

Nous avons l'insigne honneur de vous posséder parmi
nous, vous que nous vénérons comme le représentant de
l'autorité divine, le premier pasteur de ce diocèse, qui
est administré par Votre Grandeur avec une sagesse
consommée et un courage infatigable. Vous êtes venu
dans le domaine dit de Saint-Faron, pour répondre à
l'aimable invitation de Monsieur et de Madame Foucher,
qui en sont les propriétaires. Monsieur Foucher, ancien
notaire à Paris, et maire, pendant plusieurs années, du
IXe arrondissement, est d'une honorabilité qui mérite
tout éloge ; il se distingue, de plus, par une piété ferme
et sincère, au milieu de l'indifférence religieuse qui nuit

tant à nos populations. Madame Foucher, sa digne épouse, non moins pieuse que lui, se fait surtout remarquer par la bonté de son cœur. Je crois donc être l'interprète fidèle de tous ceux qui m'entourent en affirmant que Monsieur et Madame Foucher sont des chrétiens exemplaires et la providence visible de la paroisse du Plessis-Placy, par les bienfaits qu'ils répandent, chaque année, parmi les familles les plus nécessiteuses. L'église paroissiale elle-même a été, en plusieurs circonstances, l'objet de leur générosité, à la grande édification des fidèles.

C'est un motif religieux, comme vous le savez, Monseigneur, qui a guidé ces généreux bienfaiteurs dans l'invitation qu'ils vous ont faite. Dès le premier pèlerinage du diocèse de Meaux au sanctuaire de Notre-Dame de Lourdes, il y a trois ans, Monsieur et Madame Foucher ont été heureux de pouvoir se procurer une statue de l'Immaculée Conception qui a été bénite par Monseigneur l'évêque de Tarbes au lieu même de l'apparition. Transportée par la vapeur à Saint-Faron, cette statue de Notre-Dame-de-Lourdes fut aussitôt exposée publiquement à la vénération des fidèles. Un grand nombre de pèlerins sont venus des paroisses environnantes demander à la Vierge Immaculée la santé de l'âme et du corps, et nous savons que les vœux de plusieurs d'entre eux ont été exaucés. Car la sainte Vierge Marie, selon l'expression des saints Pères, est une toute-puissance suppliante, *Omnipotentia supplex*, c'est-à-dire que cette Mère incomparable obtient tout de son divin Fils par ses supplications et ses prières. Elle peut par grâce ce que Dieu peut par nature.

Alors, par un élan de foi bien louable, Monsieur et Madame Foucher ont jugé à propos de procurer à l'Immaculée Conception une demeure digne d'elle, dans leur propriété. De là, l'origine de cette belle et riche chapelle que vous êtes appelé à bénir sous le vocable de *Notre-Dame-de-Lourdes-de-Saint-Faron*. Désormais, la victime sainte y sera offerte, pour la plus grande gloire de Dieu et le salut des âmes, par l'intercession de la bienheureuse et Immaculée Vierge Marie.

Béni soyez-vous, Monseigneur, d'être venu, au nom du Seigneur, pour attirer les faveurs célestes sur les généreux bienfaiteurs de Saint-Faron ; pour raviver la foi parmi les bons habitants de cette paroisse et pour obtenir lumières, force et consolation à ces vrais serviteurs de Marie, qui se sont empressés d'assister, en grand nombre, à cette solennelle cérémonie : nous en garderons tous, prêtres et fidèles, le précieux souvenir.

Monseigneur, répondant au vénérable curé, applaudit à la pensée qui a donné naissance à ce pèlerinage. « Ceux qui vont à Lourdes en reviennent charmés, mais les Pyrénées sont loin, tous ne peuvent s'y rendre. Il était bien qu'un oratoire de Lourdes fût érigé dans notre Brie. Elle fut jadis la terre des saints : puisse la Vierge immaculée y vaincre l'indifférence et y ramener la ferveur des anciens jours ! »

Le pontife descend ensuite dans l'oratoire qu'il bénit avec son autel.

M, Perdrau prend, à son tour, la parole, à la porte de cette petite chapelle. Le docte auteur des *Dernières années de la très sainte Vierge* s'exprime ainsi :

C'est une grande bonté de votre part, Monseigneur, que de venir présider cette petite fête de famille. Vous donnez à mes parents, dont la piété a élevé cette chapelle, un témoignage d'estime et de bienveillance dont ils sont infiniment honorés, et vous comblez leurs vœux en voulant bien bénir cette chapelle et cet autel. C'est d'ailleurs une des hautes fonctions de l'Episcopat que de bénir. Lorsque le cardinal Pie, l'Evêque si regretté de Poitiers, consacrait votre illustre frère Evêque de Saint-Dié, il nous décrivait avec ces paroles magistrales que Dieu avait mises sur ses lèvres, cette magnifique fonction de l'Evêque, image du Dieu du ciel occupé à bénir, c'est-à-dire à faire passer la grâce de Dieu sur les créatures qui la représentent. La bénédiction de l'Evêque attache la grâce de Dieu à ces signes pieux; ils deviennent sous sa main non seulement des objets bénis, mais des sources spirituelles d'où la grâce s'échappe et se répand sur tous ceux qui la viennent recueillir. Cette statue de Notre-Dame bénite à Lourdes sera un signe et une source de salut pour cette maison et tout le pays. Elle rappellera aux habitants de cette contrée un fait très extraordinaire qui s'est passé de nos jours, et qui nous montre d'une façon éclatante la bonté inépuisable de Dieu sur la terre de France.

Rien de plus simple que l'histoire de Notre-Dame de Lourdes. La sainte Vierge apparait à une jeune paysanne des Pyrénées. Elle lui dit qu'elle veut voir s'établir en ce lieu un pèlerinage ; elle promet d'y attacher sa bienveillance et ses bienfaits. A la voix de Marie, ce lieu devient en peu d'années un des pèlerinages les plus fréquentés de l'Eglise catholique; des millions de fidèles accourent du monde entier, les grâces du ciel s'écoulent du rocher de Lourdes comme d'une source intarissable.

Tout dans cette histoire me parait digne et vrai : J'ai eu l'honneur de voir la pauvre paysanne à qui la Vierge était apparue, j'ai conversé longtemps avec elle. On ne pouvait trouver une âme plus simple, plus pure, plus humble. Si Dieu aime à se révéler aux tout petits, Bernadette était digne d'être choisie entre toutes. Ce que lui dit la Sainte Vierge est digne de sa bonté, car rien n'est plus digne des saints que de chercher et de procurer la gloire de Dieu. La parole de Marie a donné à son divin fils N. S. J.-C. une incomparable gloire sur le rocher de

Lourdes. Enfin les grâces de conversions, de guérisons qui s'obtiennent chaque jour à Lourdes sont dignes de la miséricorde de Dieu. A Lourdes comme à Cana, Jésus-Christ, à la voix de sa mère, laisse échapper de ses mains cette vertu miraculeuse qui constitue la dot très riche de sa divine Incarnation.

Cet ordre merveilleux de grâces a été plusieurs fois constaté par ceux qui ont autorité dans l'Eglise pour discerner les dons de Dieu. En lisant la lettre que Monseigneur l'Evêque de Tarbes écrivait encore en ce dernier temps sur les récentes guérisons et conversions obtenues devant Notre-Dame de Lourdes, tout vrai chrétien, comme vous l'êtes tous, mes frères, n'a qu'à répéter les paroles de nos livres saints : « le doigt de Dieu est ici. *Digitus Dei est hic.* » Il n'est pas étonnant que ceux qui ont été à Lourdes désirent garder de ce pèlerinage un souvenir actuel et vivant. Voilà pourquoi de nombreux sanctuaires de Notre-Dame de Lourdes se sont élevés dans le monde entier; ordinairement ils sont l'œuvre de pieux pèlerins qui au retour veulent conserver de leur voyage un saint souvenir et encore faire partager aux chrétiens, avec lesquels ils vivent, la joie et la consolation qu'ils ont recueillies au pied même de la célèbre montagne. C'est la pensée qui a présidé à l'érection de ce très modeste sanctuaire. Ceux qui l'ont élevé voudraient transporter ici quelques-unes des grâces qu'ils ont eux-mêmes obtenues. Pourquoi pas ? Cette pensée n'a rien que de très charitable et de très pratique. La Très Sainte Vierge n'étend-elle pas sa protection sur l'Eglise entière ? Quand les peintres du moyen-âge nous la présentent étendant son manteau sur tout le globe terrestre, ils ne font que traduire en une jolie image l'universalité de la bonté de Marie. Ce qu'il faut, c'est que les fidèles pensent à Marie; ce qu'il faut, c'est qu'ils soient excités à la prier, à essayer de sa miséricorde. La vue de Notre-Dame de Lourdes vous rappellera, mes frères, la puissance, la tendre maternité de la Très Sainte Vierge. Vous voudrez expérimenter par vous-mêmes cette prière qui obtient à Lourdes de si grands bienfaits. En vous mettant dévotement à genoux devant cette statue, vous inclinerez doucement la Très Sainte Vierge à vous être bonne dans le sanctuaire de Saint-Faron, comme elle est bonne à ceux qui la vont chercher dans ce sanctuaire de Lourdes.

C'est pour vous obtenir cette grâce que votre vénérable Evêque va bénir cette chapelle. Lorsqu'une source jaillit avec abondance du sein de la terre, les hommes sont habiles à en diriger les eaux; par maints conduits, ils les font couler en des bassins éloignés où l'on vient les chercher avec bonheur. Votre main, Monseigneur, va mettre en communication le sanctuaire de Lourdes et ce sanctuaire. A Lourdes, la grâce est une source; ici, elle va devenir sous votre bénédiction un ruisseau abondant où tous ceux de ce pays viendront puiser avec empressement. Ainsi soit-il.

Après cet éloquent discours, Monseigneur bénit le chemin de croix appendu aux murs de l'oratoire, et un ornement sacerdotal qui exciterait l'envie d'une cathédrale.

† † †

La procession rentre dans le parc au chant du cantique des apparitions, sous la direction d'une infatigable Augustine. L'*Ave Maria* retentit à travers les allées sinueuses, comme aux roches Massabielle dans les lacets savamment tracés qui montent de la grotte à la basilique. Le soleil se joue à travers le feuillage, la joie est dans tous les cœurs, mais surtout dans ceux de M. et de Mme Foucher qui suivent humblement le clergé.

Le cortège parvient à un Calvaire où le prélat bénit un grand christ en fonte que l'assistance salue par le cantique *Vive Jésus ! vive sa croix !*

Un peu plus loin, dans un rond-point, est **une statue de Saint-Joseph**, également en fonte, que le pontife bénit, et que la foule acclame par un cantique populaire.

Les ombres des Bénédictins n'ont-elles pas tressailli pendant que ces chants harmonieux retentissaient sous les arbres dont plusieurs ont été plantés par eux ?

Cette cérémonie, si complète dans sa variété, avait duré plus d'une heure : elle avait été fort bien conçue et menée. Les pèlerins se dispersent sous les arbres de l'avenue de Saint-Faron, pour y prendre une courte réfection. Sur une motion faite par plusieurs membres des pèlerinages diocésains à Lourdes, la récitation du rosaire et les cantiques se succèdent devant l'oratoire comme devant la grotte des Pyrénées. La piété engendre l'aumône : une quête est proposée par une âme généreuse en faveur d'un estropié mêlé aux pèlerins.

A l'intérieur du domaine de Saint-Faron, le propriétaire, dans un discours dont les pensées sont aussi délicates que les termes en sont heureux, remercie le prélat, les prêtres qui l'ont suivi et les autorités de la commune.

Monseigneur,

Permettez-moi de vous adresser tous nos remerciements de l'honneur que vous avez bien voulu nous faire en venant bénir en personne notre modeste oratoire.

Depuis trois ans que ma chère et bien-aimée femme a eu l'heureuse pensée d'amener de Lourdes à Saint-Faron l'image bénie de notre bonne mère du ciel, la Très Sainte Vierge nous a comblés de ses grâces. Plusieurs guérisons dont les preuves sont réunies dans les archives de Lourdes, des conversions plus précieuses encore ont signalé son installation parmi nous; aussi plus de douze mille pèlerins sont-ils déjà venus se prosterner à ses pieds, et son culte s'est-il étendu autour de nous de la manière la plus consolante : La bénédiction de son nouveau sanctuaire contribuera puissamment, nous en avons l'assurance, à le développer encore; grâces vous en soient rendues, Monseigneur.

Votre présence dans ces lieux qui portent le nom d'un de vos plus illustres prédécesseurs, dans ces lieux possédés pendant plusieurs siècles par des religieux de Meaux, sanctifiés par leurs prières qui devaient y préparer l'installation de la Très Sainte Vierge, fera ce qu'elle fait dans les lieux que Votre Grandeur daigne visiter, ce qu'elle a fait notamment à Lourdes dont vous avez la gloire d'avoir montré le chemin à notre diocèse, en y conduisant ses deux premiers pèlerinages si remarquables par leur belle organisation, leur piété, leur recueillement, que Lourdes les cite toujours comme des modèles; votre présence à Saint-Faron laissera dans nos campagnes les plus salutaires, les plus précieux souvenirs.

Permettez-moi, Monseigneur, d'adresser aussi nos remerciements à M. le vicaire général que nous avons été si heureux de voir vous accompagner.

A notre cher cousin, M. l'abbé Perdrau, curé de Saint-Etienne du Mont, chanoine honoraire de Paris, dont la place était marquée dans cette cérémonie, lui qui nous a fait connaître, nous a révélé avec tant de charme et d'autorité, dans ces pages si attachantes, si religieuses, si éloquentes, que nous avons tous lues et admirées, les *Dernières années de la Très Sainte Vierge* sur la terre.

A M. l'archiprêtre de Meaux, pour qui nous avons tous une si vive sympathie.

A M. le curé de Saint-Nicolas qui, plus heureux que nous, a pu s'agenouiller dans tous les sanctuaires de la Terre-Sainte et nous en a rapporté ce magnifique ouvrage rempli d'un si puissant intérêt et d'une si profonde érudition.

A M. l'aumônier de l'hospice de Meaux, ce savant si modeste pour qui l'antiquité chrétienne n'a pas de secrets dans notre diocèse, cet organisateur habile de nos beaux pèlerinages.

A notre excellent doyen, au vénérable curé de notre paroisse, à M. Benoist, maire de notre commune, à vous tous, Messieurs, qui avez bien voulu ajouter par votre concours empressé à l'éclat de cette belle cérémonie.

A vous surtout, Monseigneur, l'hommage de notre vive, profonde et respectueuse reconnaissance.

A leur tour, les hôtes du vénérable M. Foucher lui expriment leur reconnaissance pour une aussi belle manifestation religieuse. Tous, en se séparant, se promettent de revenir au *petit Lourdes* où l'on est assuré de l'accueil le plus cordial.

UN PÈLERIN MELDOIS.

Meaux. — A. Le Blondel, imprimeur-libraire de l'Evêché.

134

For Heather

Symphonies

"C'mon Mikey, I'll race ya…" Phil called back as he sped away on his skateboard. Mike's best friend, Phil was the only one besides his dad who got away with calling him "Mikey", and that was because they had been best friends forever. His dad still got away with it because the alternative could have been "Junior".

"You haven't got a prayer." Mike called back as he took off after his friend. Mike wasn't big for his age, but he wasn't the stereotypical "geek" either, even though at sixteen years old he had already earned two bachelor's degrees in Electrical and Civil Engineering and one in Applied Physics from the local college. At the same time as his father had advanced Mike's education he also did his best to see that young Mike enjoyed an otherwise normal childhood, normal for a genius at least. Mike had played Little League and joined the Boy Scouts, even though it's not so easy to make friends when your I.Q. is so far above all of your peers.

Then there was Phil. They had been friends since Mike and his dad moved to New Los Angeles, when Mike was three. Mike's mom had just died. He was feeling very alone. Phil, who was the same age, lived in the house behind theirs. They clicked from the first day that the Kellys moved in and, they had been friends ever since. Phil kept Mike grounded while Mike senior developed his son's potential. Between the two of them young Michael Colford-Kelly had turned out to be a terrific guy, and he was also a pretty good skateboarder. Just as he caught up to Phil at the end of the next block, his father called him on his cell phone.

"Hi, Junior, it's dad. I need you to come home right away. There is a real problem that I need your help with."

"Sure pops. Be right there." Mike hung up the phone and turned to Phil. "We gotta get to the treehouse." He told him. "Dad's in trouble and it's big."

"Whoa, Mikey, what's happening?"

"Not sure. About a year ago, my dad came up with these code words he wanted me to remember. He said if he ever phoned me and called me 'junior' I was to do the exact opposite of whatever he said. If I understood, I was to call him 'pops'. He just told me not to come home. Phil, I gotta find out what's goin' on! I can do that from the treehouse. Only we haveta go from your place."

The Kellys called it a treehouse, but that was a euphemism. Mike had designed it when he was studying engineering at the community college. It was a self-contained enclosed structure at the top of the ancient oak tree in their backyard. It was designed as Mike's personal "command centre". It was also designed so that if they wanted to, someone might have lived there in relative comfort.

Hidden within the folds of the tree were the pipes for

plumbing and power cables. Inside Mike had built a command centre for all of his activities, that included computers connected by cables and Wi-Fi to the house mainframe. From the treehouse he could tap into all of the house computers and activate their webcams. He could also access the house security system's cameras.

The old oak was massive. It must have been at least two hundred years old. Its trunk was meters wide. Access to the treehouse, nestled in its broad branches, could be attained via an enclosed conduit from the outside of the tree at ground level (if one knew where the concealed hatch was), or by a tunnel that ran from the basement of the Kelly home. It was obvious that the whole system was designed by a genius. What was also obvious was that, that genius was, at the time, also a fourteen year old boy.

Since its original construction, with the permission of Phil's parents, Mike had extended the tunnel from his house over to theirs, so that Phil could access the treehouse, unseen, as well. It was this access that Mike used to get to his "fortress".

A quick examination of the system showed that someone was attempting to access the house mainframe, without success. Without server access the treehouse computers were invisible from the house. Mike polled the house computers. In his father's study his dad was at his computer. Three men in black suits were standing around him. They weren't aware that Mike had tapped in. From the conversation, he could tell that they were attempting to coerce his father into granting them access to the mainframe.

Mike senior's lip was bleeding and both eyes were blackened, blood was running down his chin. His hair was a mess with clotted blood. They had really worked him over, but still he would not comply. In the family room there was a young woman, also in a black suit, using the computer that was attached to the entertainment system, in an attempt to hack the mainframe.

Back in his father's office one man, who was obviously leading the group, was still trying to get his father to cooperate. "Look, Dr. Kelly, we are goin' to get what we came for eventually. Why not make it easy on yerself and give us access to your data."

"So you can sell it to the highest bidder?" Mike senior asked, hotly.

The man struck him in the back of the head with the butt of his gun. "If you had only been smart about it when we approached you in the beginnin', you could've had a share of those profits. To certain people this force field of yers is worth billions!" he drawled. "You could have asked for millions, even tens of millions of dollars and we would have given it to you willingly. Now we're forced to get tough. I am sure that I don't have to spell it out for you.

"When yer son gets home either you'll give us what we want or Bubba, here, will start to work on him. He's got a whole repertoire of things that he can do to a kid that always has their folks singin' like canaries in the end." The very large man, to whom the leader was referring, gave Mike's dad a sinister grin.

In spite of his multiple injuries, and the fact that the act hurt him immensely, Mike Kelly smiled. "Except my son is never coming home." he told them. "When you forced me to call him, I gave him a code. I told him that it wasn't safe here, and that he should get as far away as he could. You'll never find him."

The younger Mike checked the cameras in the basement. Although the place was trashed and men were still searching, they hadn't yet found the camouflaged entrance to the system mainframe hidden down there, even with ultrasensitive sound and thermal sensing equipment to listen for the sounds of the hard drives, and search for the thermal signatures of the servers.

On Mike's back-up monitor there was one word "SCORCH" in large red letters. Mike responded with the word "ENGAGE". Mike knew that the servers wouldn't make a sound that the men, with all their super spy equipment, could hear. However, when the all the servers in the room came online at once, their thermal level might rise to the point where they could register on the thermal equipment, but that couldn't be helped. By the time the men in black realized what was happening, it would be too late.

Even as their instruments detected the rise in the temperature, pointing them to the location of the server room, the transfer of the data was being completed. All data had been backed up to a secure system at Kennedy Air Base in Vermont, where one of his dad's best friends, Colonel Urnbreach, was in command. The final command of the SCORCH protocol was to send an electromagnetic pulse through the entire house.

Only the security system was (he hoped) shielded from its effect. It had a separate system that was connected by cables to the tree house. This should allow Mike to continue seeing what was happening inside.

The EMP burst hit everything in its range at once, and everywhere in the house, every electronic device went blank. The earbuds of the men and women in the black suits went dead, as did their cell phones. Even their watches died. The screens on all the computers went blank and did not re-boot.

Mike called up the shielded security camera in his father's study. Just out of the camera's field of vision, he heard someone demanding an explanation for the events.

"Dr. Kelly, would you kindly explain to me just what the hell is goin' on here." To Mike's frustration, the shielding had proved less than adequate; the security camera was damaged. Still, Mike heard the man's gentle southern accent become a thick southern drawl. "Get these computers back up and on-line now, or I assure you that we will find yer son, an' when we do, we'll make y'all real sorry that you did this. I promise you that."

"You will never find my son. I took care of that," Kelly senior told him defiantly. "He has more brains than all of you, times ten. He's half way to safety by now, and when he gets there, he will be protected. I can guarantee you of that." Kelly smiled again. "As for the computers, they are all fried beyond recovery. Whatever you hoped to get out of me is gone. It is out of your reach forever."

After his final announcement, Mike's father sat stoically

silent. The man struck him again in the back of the head. He didn't move. The man put his gun to Mike senior's head. Mike wished that he could swing the camera around to see the man's face, but movement was controlled by the now-dead computer system, as was the ability to record the unfolding events. As the man pressed the gun into his father's skull, he noticed the distinctive tattoo of modified yin/yang symbols in a triangular pattern on the back of the man's left wrist just above his watch.

"One last time, Kelly; tell me how to get the system back on-line," the man shouted, speaking with his heavy southern drawl. His father didn't move or speak. After a brief pause, the man in the black suit squeezed the trigger. Mike watched his dad's head explode. He was down the access tube faster than he had ever gone before. There, he ran into Phil, who he'd asked to wait below. The tunnel from the house had carried the sound of the gunshot, and his friend had guessed what had transpired. He blocked Mike as he headed for the tunnel.

"They'll kill you, too!" he said in a forced whisper, as he blocked Mike's progress. "We gotta go. YOU gotta go! They're gonna be looking for you. They'll eventually get the idea to check out here." Mike's first impulse was countered by his friend's counsel and he struggled to calm himself.

"Ya, you're right, but there is one last thing that I need to do." He returned to the treehouse and accessed the tunnel entrance controls. The main control was on his system and not dependant on the house computers. "When my dad started to worry about the possibility, that what just happened would happen, he didn't tell me what it was. Only, I guessed that there was real danger. So I made some modifications to the main tunnel and the treehouse," he told Phil. "Go home. I'll meet you there. Stay well away from the tunnel, once you're clear of it."

Phil nodded and left. Mike took a last look around the treehouse. He grabbed what he called a "go bag" (he took the name from and FBI drama on the holovision) from under the desk. On the computer's keyboard he typed: "Mike's Revenge: 20 seconds: GO" and hit ENTER. He then hit the switch to release the latch on the hidden tunnel entrance in the basement of his house. Lastly, he jumped down the fire pole in the access tube that he had originally put in, "just for fun", and ran as fast as he could to Phil's house.

In the Kelly basement, the two agents saw the door to the tunnel open a crack, but they didn't enter, choosing, as Mike had hoped, to call upstairs for back-up. Three more agents joined them and the four men and a woman headed toward the treehouse. They were about half way to the old oak when the twenty second countdown ended.

By then Mike had arrived in Phil's basement. He closed the door to the tunnel and triggered the lock just as the countdown reached zero. Where Mike had acquired the ordinance, he never told anyone, but all at once, the whole Kelly backyard went up in a fireball. The oak tree was reduced to ash, and any evidence of the tunnel extension to Phil's house was obliterated.

"All the same," Mike said to the Flicksteins, "you need to be elsewhere, right now – just in case they check over here.

They might already know who my friends are." When they didn't move right away, Mike pleaded with them. "Please, you really need to be somewhere else, as a family. Make it look like you haven't seen me all day."

"What about you?" Philip senior asked. "How can we help? Can't we call the police?"

"Check your phones. You can't. They'll have seen to that. Whoever they are, they kill at will. That means that they have some nasty clout. That's why you can't help me. Right now, I'm hot, nuclear-type hot! I probably just killed two or more bad guys who may just have been government 'black-ops'. Anyone caught helping me, will end up very dead. My dad and I set up all kinds of things. I've got money and even an expertly-made fake ID."

"Still," Philip Flickstein insisted, "can we at least drop you somewhere?"

Mike at first was very resistant, but when Marian and young Phil both added their voices to the elder Flickstein's entreaty, he relented. "Gardendale Estates is only ten minutes away by pod. Beth Shalom synagogue is right next to St. Aloysius church. I think that their Shabbat services begin soon. What better alibi for you all than going to Friday evening shul?"

The Flicksteins agreed. As they pulled out of the garage Mike hid in the back of their pod under a blanket. Philip senior purposefully didn't activate the privacy circuit on the windows, in case, they were already being watched. Eleven minutes later they arrived at Temple Beth Shalom where they all got out, except for Mike. He waited in the pod until after the services finished. As the Flicksteins returned to their pod, Mike slipped out into the parking lot. He was wearing one of young Phil's kippahs, and hoped that, if they were being watched, he would blend into the crowd of worshippers heading home.

Whatever the case, he successfully made it to the back edge of the parking area where he hopped a small wall. He ducked down and removed the kippah. Staying behind the cover that the wall provided, Mike made his way to the street behind, and from there, he found his way to St. Aloysius Gonzaga church. As he expected, the church was open.

Inside, he stopped, for a moment, to say a prayer for his father before heading to the door that led to the rectory. He rang the bell, and it was answered by the new pastor, Father Don. Father Don knew Mike from his previous assignment at St. Anselm's Parish in Mike's neighbourhood. He was not totally surprised by Mike's appearance.

"What happened?" he asked. Mike senior had spoken with Father Don some time ago, and had asked him to look out for Mike, should the need arise.

"He's dead, Father. Dad is dead. Some people in black suits were in our house. One of them shot him in the head."

"Did you SCORCH the place?" Father Don asked. Mike looked at the priest with surprise. "Your dad asked me to look out for you. He told me about SCORCH, and that if you did it, then you would probably need help getting out of town."

"Will you help me, Father?" he asked.

"Of course, what do you need, money, transportation?"

"I have money, Father. My dad set it up a while back. But I'll need help getting a mag-lev out of town. I need to get to Uncle Rob and Uncle James, in Vermont. These people will be watching for me, and," he paused for a moment, "also, I need to go to confession, Father. I did something very bad." Father Don led Mike into his office.

A side of him that few parishioners at St. Al's or St. Anselm's ever knew about, was Father Don's love of theatre. It seems that he was quite the thespian during his college days, before entering the Jesuits. If people learned of it he told them that it was why his homilies were so entertaining. It was his flair for the dramatic. Now his talents were being put to another use. Within thirty minutes, Mike's own father wouldn't have known him.

In spite of Mike's insistence that he could afford the fare, Father Don insisted on paying for his train tickets to Vermont. He reasoned that if anyone were looking for Mike, there would be no red flags going up on the ticket purchase. The ticket was purchased on the pastor's credit card in Mike's assumed name.

The trip was not a direct one. Again, the priest reasoned, that Vermont-bound trains in particular would be watched. Also, the next one was only leaving at 8:00 AM, the following day. Instead, Mike was to take the 9:00 PM mag-lev to Louisville, Kentucky that night, where he would wait in the lounge to connect with another mag-lev leaving for Bangor,

Maine at 3:00 AM. From there, he would double back to Burlington, Vermont. Father Don reasoned that there was a greater chance that this route would go unobserved. As they stood on the mag-lev platform, the priest gave Mike some final instructions.

"Right now, you don't look at all like your ID card. The moment this train pulls out of the station head to the jigs, clean off all of that makeup. Don't throw away the wig and the mask on the train. Toss them in a Louisville Station washroom trash bin. Just make sure that you look like you before the conductor comes round to check the tickets. I booked you into a car half way up the train. That should give you just enough time."

Mike nodded his assent at each instruction. When Father Don finished he asked, "Father, where did you learn this stuff?" To which Father Don replied, "Let's just say that I wasn't always a priest." He smiled at some secret joke. "God go with you Michael. I'll call your Uncle Rob and tell him that you're on your way, and that he needs to arrange your safe retrieval in Burlington. Remember, they may have people there, too."

Mike nodded his assent, again. "Thank you, Father. And watch your back. If they find out that it was you who helped me, it could be bad."

"Trust in God, Mike," Father Don said. He gave him a hug and then turned him toward his car, just as the final boarding call sounded.

At Kennedy base, Colonel Urnbreach knocked on the

office door of Dr. Robert Gauthier, the head of the base hospital. He didn't wait for a reply, but stuck his head in the door. "You wanted to see me, Rob?" he asked.

"Yes, Jim, please come in." The colonel entered and sat in the chair that Dr. Gauthier offered. "This is what I wanted to see you about." He handed the colonel a file folder. "Mike Kelly is dead."

"I figured that might be the case," Colonel Urnbreach replied, "when my system received a message that SCORCH had been activated. I haven't checked the status, yet."

"I did, the data check confirms that everything made it. Young Mike, also, got away successfully. I got a call from a priest in Gardendale. Mike'll be in Burlington at 06:00 tomorrow. The priest, a Father Don Fitzgerald, says that he thinks that someone might be watching the station. He wanted to be sure that we would be there to greet him."

The Colonel grunted his agreement. "I'll take a detail personally. Don't worry, Rob, your godson will be kept safe; but what about the long term? They will come looking, eventually."

Dr. Gauthier indicated the file folder in the colonel's hands. "That's what that is about."

Jim Urnbreach opened the folder. "You have to be kidding!" he said, after seeing the first page. "He won't be seventeen until the end of July. He's too young to enlist."

"Not if his legal guardian, me, signs for him, and, if

you ok it as well, there will be no problem."

"Rob, unless he's grown a whole lot since Easter, he'll never pass the physical." The doctor just smiled at that. "Ok, so you'll pass him. What then? What do I do with him?"

"Send him to basic," the doctor said matter-of-factly. "He may be small, but he is fit. He should make it through."

"Ok, again, that's the summer. What happens after that? By rights, we should be shipping him off to the Central American conflict. Are you suggesting that we send your godson to fight against the drug cartel's mercs?"

"No," the doctor continued in the same *I've got it all figured out* voice, "we send him to school." He looked at his friend and commanding officer. "The only reason that he isn't already doing graduate studies is that stupid 'University Lottery'.

"Instead of making prospective students take entrance exams, the mucky-mucks convinced their congressional stooges to vote in that lottery thing that they have in Europe, 'Where every student has the same chance.' How long is it going to take for the investigation that proves that the fix is in here, in the States? The people with big money go to grad school no matter how mediocre they may be, while geniuses like young Mike sit waiting on a lottery every six months.

"Well, now he can get in to one of the places reserved for Forces personnel. He'll be safely out of the way, and when he's done, the Air Force gets one whiz bang officer and researcher!" The doctor smiled at his own plan.

"That's all well and good, but his test scores will surely qualify him for Flight School." Jim Urnbreach told the doctor.

"So? You know that he helped his father design those simulators in Hanger B? He's been flying the heck out of them since he was ten! He can fly, Jim. You can count on that. And you can defer his Flight School till next summer, if you think it's necessary, after his first year at Yale or Harvard or wherever you send him. Knowing him, he'll probably be writing his thesis by then. He'll have loads of time to wow them over in Sector C."

Colonel Urnbreach gave in. As he picked up his pen to sign the forms, he looked at his friend. "He still might not go for this." he said.

"What choice does he have?"

"None, I suppose. I see that you have used his mother's name, 'Colford' here."

The doctor nodded. "Yes, I thought it would be safer, and it's still legal."

"Let's just hope that he agrees to both proposals." the colonel said.

At 05:50 hours, the mag-lev train from Bangor, Maine pulled into the Burlington station. Cautiously, Mike detrained. He looked around for any sign of "Uncle Rob" or "Uncle Jim". He couldn't see either of them.

As it happened, Colonel Urnbreach had been delayed at the base by a sudden phone call, supposedly, from the

Pentagon. It had seemed strange to him that the call came in at 05:00 hours, but was of a very pedestrian nature. The only reason that he could think of was that the "men in black suits" had guessed Mike's itinerary and were hoping to delay the Colonel in his office long enough to grab the boy at the station before anyone else could meet him. The Burlington station was a good forty-five minute drive from the base. Colonel Urnbreach needed to get on the road right away to arrive before the train did. That didn't happen.

When the call ended at 05:20, Urnbreach was certain that it was a set-up, arranged by the unknown individuals chasing Mike across the country. He needed to increase his odds. He already had arranged for the men of his detail to use their civilian vehicles for the trip so that things wouldn't be so obvious. They would enter the station parking through different gates. Everyone was to be wearing civilian clothes. The only give away would be, if anyone noticed, that his detail was so heavily armed. So their major weapons were in special travel cases, designed to fall way in a hurry. Hopefully no one at the station had ever seen one before.

The colonel jumped into the lead car and ordered his men to push the speed. "No accidents, but move it! If you get stopped by a cop show him your ID and tell him that it's a Homeland Security op. If he argues, show him your gun, and bring him along. I'll fix it later." Fortunately for everyone, and for the operation, no one was stopped, but the group reached the station just at 06:00 hours.

Mike had also been lucky. His pursuers had not actually guessed his plans. Though they had put men in the station just in case, the contingent was minimal. They had several possible destinations to cover. Despite the fact that he hadn't slept all night, Mike had his wits about him. He had noticed a possible pursuer out of the corner of his eye. He was wearing the exact same black suit. Just in time, Mike ducked back into the car. He made his way down the car to its front end, passing through the connecting door to the next car. Moving from car to car he made his way to the front end of the train.

Mike went to the conductor and asked if anyone had turned in a pair of lost eyeglasses. The motherly woman was most helpful, and showed him a box destined for the "Lost and Found" department. Mike chose the thickest, nerdiest pair that he could see. He feigned great relief, and thanked the conductor profusely. Donning the kippah that Phil had loaned, him he then exited the train right in front of the man in the black suit he had noticed from his car.

Mike passed within a foot of the man he guessed was searching for him. The coke-bottle glasses made it difficult to avoid running into him, but Mike reasoned that the more details he presented the seeker, the greater the chance that the agent wouldn't be able to put them all together with the photo that he had most likely been given.

His next move was equally gutsy. Mike had been to Vermont several times with his father. He knew the station by heart, so navigating virtually blind was not too difficult. He bought a paper at the newsstand, sat down on the bench outside the ticket office, and waited. He was sure that his pursuers would not expect him to sit there in plain sight reading the paper while they were looking for him; so that is just what he did. It turned out that Father Don wasn't the only good actor. Mike worked at holding a newspaper that he couldn't read at, what he believed to be, the correct distance, turning the pages at believable intervals. Every so often, he looked over the top of his glasses at the gate to see if one of his uncles had arrived.

At 05:55 Mike took a look over his paper to see one of the men in the black suits walking over to him.

"Hey kid…" the man began, "was there a kid on the train, about your age, not Jewish? He would have been a bit of an egghead type, probably a nerdy kid." Obviously they had been briefed on Mike's capabilities and had assumed the rest.

Considering his disguise, Mike surmised that the man was probably trying to flatter him by suggesting that he didn't look like a nerd. Mike answered him with his best imitation of Phil's Brooklyn-born grandfather.

"Not in the car I was in." he said, and then returned his attention to the newspaper, turning the page to emphasize that the conversation was over. The man in the black suit returned to his search none the wiser.

At one minute after six, he saw the colonel enter with four men dressed like businessmen. Another four "businessmen" entered the platform at the other end. Each was carrying some sort of briefcase. Mike nearly jumped. He was sure that nine commuters in the train station, that early on a Saturday morning, would be a dead giveaway. But the men in black suits didn't bat an eyelash. Mike waited until two of his pursuers snuck onto the train to look for him. He then ambled his way over to the colonel and offered him the newspaper, as if he had asked to see it. "Uncle Jim." was all he said.

James Urnbreach was a true soldier. He never batted an eyelash. He took the paper, and seemingly thanked the young stranger who gave it to him. What he actually said was, "By the gate, brown shirt, call him Uncle George and go with him." As Mike followed the instructions, Urnbreach opened the paper and continued to speak softly into it. Within moments, he and his squad were back in their cars and returning to base. Mike rode with the Colonel.

As the train pulled out of the station fifteen minutes later, the men in black suits reported back that "the Kelly kid was not on the train". In response they were ordered to wait for the one that was coming directly from New Los Angeles, that afternoon. Many years later, Mike learned that they had manned the station for a month trying to catch him, and had finally concluded that he hadn't gone to Vermont.

"So, there was some adventure this morning?" Rob Gauthier asked as he and the Colonel shared a drink in his living room that evening.

The Colonel was sitting with his feet up and a glass of Rob Gauthier's best scotch in his hand. "A little intrigue, but your godson handled himself extremely well. He's a lot more than just an egghead that young man." Jim Urnbreach was impressed. "He saw the operatives, kept his head, and outsmarted them until we showed up. He then found a way to make contact unobserved. As far as we could tell, we got in, picked him up, and got out again without these villains being any the wiser. I'd like to think that they are still sitting on the platform waiting for him to show up." They both chuckled at the image that, that thought presented.

"But what happens now?" As they were speaking, Mike had joined them in the living room. "Is there any way that I can call my friend Phil and his family? They risked a lot to get me to St. Aloysius. I really would like to let them know that I'm ok, but if they are being watched, their phones might be bugged. I don't want to put them in any more danger."

Urnbreach thought about it for a moment. "I can arrange for a friend of mine stationed at El Toro to drop by for a visit. He'll bring them a secure tablet. You'll be able to have a conversation with your friends and let them know that you're alright. Just make sure that they tell absolutely no one else. If they are being watched then, more than likely, they won't be the only ones."

Mike brightened up until another thought occurred to him. "Do you know any more about what happened with my dad?"

The doctor took a deep breath, as much to give himself a chance to collect his thoughts before his reply as anything else. "At first, there was a report that he committed suicide because authorities discovered that he was selling secrets to foreign powers, but the Colonel made a few calls and the Pentagon immediately denied that accusation."

The doctor was trying to be as succinct as he could as he delivered the bad news. "Next, someone tried to accuse you of killing your father, claiming that the conflagration in the backyard was a failed attempt at torching the house to cover your crime. That one didn't fly too far either, especially when the LAPD discovered that your dad recently installed a shielded backup system onto the security cameras. The shielding was done hastily, so it wasn't perfect. There was some data corruption, but the recording definitely shows someone else shooting your father. What it doesn't show is your presence anywhere on the premises. So you're in the clear. Right now, it is a homicide by 'persons unknown'."

Mike let out a long breath, suddenly realizing that he had been holding his breath as the doctor had recounted the various details. Dr. Gauthier continued, "The authorities are, officially, still looking for you, but you are now being considered as a potential victim on the run, or a missing person. The FBI is involved, in case you have been kidnapped. We won't disabuse them right away. Your disappearance needs to stand beyond any investigation."

The Colonel picked up the narrative, "My friends at the Pentagon also learned a few more things. To support their story about your dad selling out, whoever they are, they deposited ten million dollars into a 'findable' bank account in your father's name. The good news there is that, since he has been cleared of their fake charges, they can't reclaim that money. As no wrong-doing can be connected to the money, it becomes a part of his estate. After all the taxes are paid everything goes into a trust fund for you."

"To be honest," Mike said, "I don't want it. It comes from the people that killed my dad. He was all the family that I had left."

"Well, if you still feel that way, when you are old enough to make your own decisions, you can do what you will with whatever is left after the taxes," the doctor told him. "For now, at least, you can take comfort that the ones who tried to frame him failed. His good name is safe. Also," Dr. Rob added, "they are out several million dollars, and still have no idea where you are or where his research is. As to family, you still have us," he said indicating the Colonel and himself.

"And that is a real comfort, really," Mike told them earnestly. "I owe both of you a lot. I'm sure that my dad would thank you if he could."

Colonel Urnbreach looked at Mike earnestly. "Like Dr. Rob said, you're family. We look after our family. Though, one thing I should mention. Since you signed those forms this afternoon, I am now also your commanding officer. In private we're family, but outside these walls it is military discipline."

Mike snapped to attention, and saluted "Yes sir, Colonel, sir!" he said, with exaggerated seriousness, breaking into a smile immediately afterward. "I understand, Uncle Jim."

"I dunno," the colonel said, "we might be in for a lonnnnng hitch," but he smiled, too.

"Tell him what happens with his enlistment," Rob told the colonel.

"Well, you took the oath, so starting next Monday you will be given the usual tests to place you. None of us here doubt that you will qualify for the Military University program, which means that you will be able to go to grad school in the fall, if that is what you want. In the meantime, you will report to Sector G, here on the base, for six weeks of basic training.

"That might be the hardest part. The training officers are supposed to be tough on the new recruits, but the doctor, here, is sure that you can handle it. You will undoubtedly qualify for Flight School. I highly recommend that you take it. It's a three month program, which I'm sure you'll ace. Obviously, as the university term begins before the end of Flight School in Sector C, we'll arrange for you to return on weekends throughout the school year to finish up. This will mean that you will be in at least three different class-groups. Please try not to make all of them look too bad. We don't want all of our flight squadrons hating your guts at the same time," he smiled at Mike again.

Mike smiled back. "I'll try to go easy on them, but you know how I get when I'm in the simulator," he said.

"A very long hitch… oh, and remember – you're Mike Colford now, just Colford. Michael Colford-Kelly is officially 'missing'."

In an office in Washington, the man with the tattooed hand met with the remaining men and women in black suits from the Los Angeles fiasco. "Do we have any idea where he might be?" he asked.

A young blond man responded: "No, sir, there have been no reports of sightings. He doesn't appear to be in New

Los Angeles, nor did he arrive in Vermont. We've had teams watching around the clock. We hacked the security cams, but found nothing. He's in the wind. We've dropped hints with the FBI so that they will check out any other possibilities. Unfortunately, he had no other family, but, his father had a great many friends. He could have gone to any one of them."

"Keep me informed. What news on the recovery of our money?"

A dark haired older woman spoke up, "It's gone! Someone moved very quickly. Once our cover about foreign entities was debunked, a federal judge ruled that it is a part of the estate. We can't touch it without exposing the front organisation."

The tattooed man was not pleased. "That's just great. Kelly is exonerated and we can't get our money back. Worse, the kid will get it! Have the locals found our agents that were in the tunnel?"

"Yes, but they haven't been able to identify them. It appears that all five were right by one of the ordinance packs when the whole place went up. The coroner can only say that there were five of them. They still don't even know what gender yet. One piece of bad news is that they found their weapons. That raised some eyebrows, that, along with the fact that they were in the tunnel at all. The local law enforcement officers are asking some very pointed questions. The local news people have picked up on it as well."

"Assessment?" the man asked.

"Even with all that," a young redheaded man began, "our exposure was minimal. They have questions, but no answers. The only people who might guess why we were there, also have a vested interest in our success. They may be disappointed that we didn't succeed, but they aren't about to start talking. It isn't in their interest."

"Finally, some good news. What about the data. Did the kid destroy it?"

The redheaded man answered again. "Unknown, but it is unlikely. We have intelligence that says he actually worked with his father on a lot of his research. It could be that he might eventually be able to finish his father's work. That may be important to him, especially in light of the manner of his father's death."

"Ok, then we keep lookin' for the kid," the man instructed. "I want him found. And I want you to get our medical people prepared, not like with his old man. I don't want to be told at the last minute that they aren't available. When we find him, that kid is goin' to talk."

By mid-July, Mike was sure that he would be glad to get away from the base in September. Basic was tough. The drill instructors rode him hard just because he was the youngest, and because he was small. By the end of the six weeks, he hadn't grown much taller, but he had definitely grown. Mike worked extra hard and had earned the respect of both his instructors and fellow recruits. Finally, the hazing and dirty tricks had stopped.

Flight school was another story. In the third week of

July, as Colonel Urnbreach recommended, Mike moved over to Sector C for Flight School. Of course, he already knew the math. He had to know it when he worked with his dad designing the simulators. As he excelled in the classroom, he became very popular, especially with the female candidates, most of whom were less reticent to ask for his help when they needed it. Eventually, all but the most macho male recruits were asking Mike to check their assignments and give them tips on both mathematics and strategies.

As Urnbreach expected, it was when they moved into the simulators that things changed. Those who were his friends in the theory section, hung in for what they could learn when they saw how he excelled in the combat simulations. The few who had eschewed his aid during the theory really resented his prowess in the simulator. It didn't help, at all, when the first cuts from the program were made, and three members of that particular minority were sent back to the ranks. Those cuts also produced one unforeseen benefit for Mike.

It happened on the night that the cuts were announced. Mike and a group of the successful candidates were returning from celebrating their success. As they were making for their respective male or female barracks, they ran into the three male members of the class who had been dropped. Jake Malachy, one of the larger recruits, was particularly drunk. He and his friends had been out drowning their sorrows when they came across Mike and his friends on their way home. As they met on the tarmac behind Sector C Malachy proceeded to demonstrate his weakness for strategy.

The moment that he noticed Mike among the others,

he moved to intercept him, blocking Mike's path. "You, Colford, smart ass, it's time someone took you down a peg," he announced just before he swung wildly. The move caught Mike off guard, but Malachy's inebriated state really limited his aim and he only caught Mike with a glancing blow. Malachy straightened up and charged again, but Mike, being under age, hadn't been drinking. He easily avoided his attacker's second attempt, and his third. He soon tired of Malachy's repeated attacks. Dodging Malachy's fourth swing he stepped into its wake and answered with a blow of his own to Malachy's kidney that staggered the larger man. Without waiting for him to recover, Mike hit him twice more. The third blow was enough to lay him out. That was the end of any further confrontation. Malachy's buddies picked him up and half-dragged him back to their new barracks.

After congratulating Mike for putting Malachy in his place, as if in response to some secret signal, all his classmates began to disperse. In short order, Mike found himself alone, or so he thought until he noticed her. Standing a short way off was Jerri Linton, a young-looking nineteen-year-old female candidate. Jerri had just barely made the cut, largely in part because of Mike's help, and she decided that she wanted to show her appreciation.

As a young genius at the local college, Mike had been used to the female students treating him like a child – a prodigy, but a child. After completing basic training, Mike's physique had filled out a great deal which gave him a much more mature appearance. That was enough for Jerri. The actual three year age difference didn't make any difference for her. She stepped forward and took Mike by the hand.

"Come here," she ordered playfully, "I've got something to show you."

"Ok…" Mike answered hesitantly, "…what is it?"

"You'll see," Jerri answered playfully, "I guess you could call it 'gratitude'." When Mike hesitated, looking off towards his barracks she added, "Didn't you hear? Captain Latrobe gave all the successful candidates an extended curfew tonight. We've got hours yet."

Jerri led Mike across the tarmac and over towards Hanger C. They passed the hanger and continued on to the storeroom behind. Mike was still wondering what Jerri had in mind. To his surprise, when she turned the handle, the storeroom door opened. Mike believed that all storage rooms in that area were supposed to be locked. Then as the door opened, Mike was reminded that this was the place where they stored the unused cots and mattresses. It was not high security. As they entered, he saw that one bed was not stacked with the others. It had been made up with a mattress and sheets.

Jerri slipped her hand out of his and walked over to the bed. Her hand dropped to her waist, and she unzipped her skirt, and undid the button. As the skirt slid to the floor, Mike couldn't help but notice that those weren't regulation skivvies that Jerri was wearing. As she turned back towards him, Mike guessed that at least one of his many fantasies was probably about to come true. She placed her arms around his neck and kissed him passionately. With her body pressed close, Jeri could feel his body respond to her embrace.

All at once, Mike thought he was going to pass out. At

one and the same time, he was more aroused than he had ever been, and he was also terrified out of his wits. Did she know that he was a virgin? Could he live up to Jerri's expectations? As she peeled off her last piece of clothing, he was sure that he was going to lose it right there.

Somehow Jerri realized his predicament. She put her arms around his neck again, but didn't pull him close. She stroked his hair, making soothing sounds in his ears. Mike relaxed just enough to bring himself back from the edge. He slid his arms around her and pulled her close. Jerri reached down and grasped the hem of his t-shirt, pulling it upwards. She danced him toward the bed…

It was just before their extended curfew when their reveries ended, and they both rushed to dress. Mike couldn't help but notice that Jerri had neglected to put on her non-regulation underwear. As she kissed him good night outside the storage shed she said, "I think I still owe you a great deal of thanks" then she smiled. "We may have to do this again – often." Still smiling, she kissed him again, slipping her thong into his hands. They then both had to sprint back to their respective barracks to make their curfew.

Mike entered the barracks just as the sergeant called for lights out. As the darkness fell in the room, Mike had just enough time to notice the grins on the faces of all his bunkmates. He knew that he was in for a ribbing the next morning. He didn't care. What had just happened in the storage room was more exciting than anything he had ever experienced in his life.

As it was, any kidding that he had to endure was made up for when as he headed towards his "plane" the next day. Out of the blue, Jerri grabbed him and pulled him out of everyone's view. She kissed him passionately. "Just so you know that I wasn't making an empty promise last night" she said. She kissed him again, quickly, and rushed off to her simulator. Mike had to work very hard to keep his mind on his flying that morning. The previous night's adventure "in paradise" and the encounters that followed set the pattern for Mike's sexual behaviour for the next fifteen years.

The next time he chatted with Phil, Mike was still beaming: "I never imagined that that would happen here." He told him over their secure connection the following evening. Phil smiled at the story he recounted.

"So much for the good Catholic boy," Phil said. "You dropped your surname and your fidelity at the same time?"

"Easy for you to say," Mike countered. "You've been dating for the past two years. This happened for me all at once. It took me by surprise. I mean, have you ever gotten laid?"

"Yeah, Mike, you know I have. And to tell the truth, the only reason that I am not getting any right now is your fault."

Mike did his best estimate of a double take at the screen. "My fault? What'd I do?"

"You remember when we went to Beth Shalom Synagogue in Gardendale so that you could get to St. Aloysius? Well, dad fell in love with the community. We joined the synagogue. We practice there every weekend, and we're involved in all their activities," Phil told Mike. "But it is more than that. Rabbi Glick told me that he thinks that I might make a good rabbi, and that's got me thinking about it. So if it is possible that I might actually become a rabbi then I should start behaving more like it, shouldn't I?"

"But rabbis aren't like priests." Mike countered, "They can get married."

"It is more than just that, Mike. It's the integrity of a man of God. One thing that our faiths have in common is a moral code of conduct that includes a sexual integrity. Following that moral code is a part of the discernment process that I need to be faithful to. I find that to be a sobering thought."

Mike thought about that for a moment. He found that he had to agree with his friend's point of view. It did sober him up for a moment, but he brightened up again. "Well, at least I'm not thinking about becoming a rabbi," he said with a grin. Then becoming serious again for a moment he added, "I'm actually glad for you, Phil. Keep me up-to-date on things. If this is what you decide is for you, I'll be pulling for you."

When September came, Jerri was very sorry to see Mike leave for Yale. The night before he left, they met in the storage shed one last time. As they were preparing to return to their respective barracks Jerri turned to Mike, putting her arms around his neck, she looked into his eyes and asked, "Do you love me?"

For a brief instant, Mike considered his answer

carefully. He decided to answer truthfully: "I really like you, Jerri, a lot." he told her, "But, no, I'm not in love with you. These last few weeks with you have been super great, but it was what it was. I can't make any more of it."

As he was speaking, Mike was sure that he could see a look of relief come over Jerri's face. She let out a sigh, "I am glad to hear you say that. You have been great with me ever since the beginning of flight school. I just hope that I can keep up with things without you. I don't want to wash out. I will miss you, though, and not just because of the help you have given me with school. Ever since that first night, our time together here has been fantastic. You're a natural between the sheets. Yes, I will miss you!" She kissed him passionately one last time, and then together they heaved their bed on top of the nearest pile and slipped out of the shed.

Without his ongoing help and advice Jerri did eventually wash out of Flight School. But if he thought that his first experience with Jerri was great, Graduate School was Mike's idea of heaven. He found the mental challenge exhilarating. Although he was studying applied physics, he added a couple of graduate level courses in electrical engineering. For him, they fit together perfectly. He lived in the dorms while he was studying, but returned to the base periodically to officially complete his flight training. One of the benefits of grad school was that he was stimulated enough by his academics that he could ease up in the simulators, and so he alienated fewer classmates.

At school, Mike wore his working blues to class. He cut quite a figure in uniform, and since he had kept up his physical training, he easily turned the heads of a great number of undergraduate co-eds. As many female undergrads on campus were closer to his age, Mike enjoyed a whole host of new adventures. Though he was always careful never to play around with any of the female students in the classes he tutored as a teaching assistant. Fortunately for his academic career, his studies still took first place, but his extra-curricular activities were a new and very pleasurable experience. Mike very quickly learned the art of seduction, and gained a reputation among the co-ed undergrads.

As Dr. Gauthier and the newly-promoted General Urnbreach predicted, Mike finished his Master's degree in sixteen months, following which the Air Force gave him permission to continue onto the Doctorate level. He argued successfully that most Master's students in applied physics took at least three years to complete both the classes and the thesis. If Mike could complete his doctorate in three more years it would be a benefit to the military and probably take less than five years for both degrees. The Air Force would have a first rate physicist and Mike would be able to fulfill his potential. On July 21, 2065 Mike celebrated his twenty-first birthday by presenting General Urnbreach with a brand new doctorate in applied physics. He also gave him a problem.

Though Kennedy Air Base was officially designated an Air Force research facility, it wasn't doing any research that fit Mike Colford's new qualifications. Neither General Urnbreach nor Dr. Gauthier would be happy to see him move off base, especially because the research that was being done in his area of expertise was mostly in California. Memories of the men in the black suits immediately came into everyone's mind.

Fortunately, Mike had an answer for that problem.

"The main research that they are doing there is in particle weapons and different types of ablative armour to protect against them," he reminded General Urnbreach. "All the information that I need to complete the research my dad was doing on force shields as protection against both conventional and energy weapons is right here. Ultimately, if I finish his work, it should also end the problem with the black-suit guys. If Uncle Sam has the technology, then there is nothing for them to steal. If they still attempt to profit from the tech, then we'll have a reason to hunt them down and charge them with treason."

"You mean more reason than just because they murdered your father?" Urnbreach countered.

"Well," Mike observed, "no one seems to be doing much in that department at the moment, are they?"

The General submitted Mike's proposal to the Pentagon, and they approved it. Along with their approval, they promoted Lieutenant Michael Colford to Captain Michael Colford. Then Mike presented his Uncles with another surprise.

"Back at the very beginning of grad school I met a fellow by the name of Henry Brackenreid, you may have heard of him?" both of them had.

"He's the fellow who won the Nobel Prize in Medicine two years ago for his development of true bionic limbs that can be permanently attached, and are fully afferent and efferent,"

Rob Gauthier responded.

"In English, please, Doctor." The General pleaded.

"It means that not only do they work exactly like real limbs," Mike explained, "they can feel and react to touch and temperature. They have full functionality and sensitivity as well as being fully controllable. They are, in all senses of the word, replacement limbs."

"What does that have to do with the price of cod in Maine?" the General asked.

"I think I know," the Doctor cut in, before Mike could answer. "I recall his acceptance speech – I watched it on the internet – he thanked a school friend, who he'd been asked not to name, for invaluable assistance in figuring out the biophysics needed to bridge the gap between the human neural system and the cybernetic controls." He looked at Mike, "That was you, wasn't it?" Mike just grinned.

The General was still trying to understand what Mike was asking for. "…and what does that have to do with your being on this base?"

"Biophysics wasn't all I had to research in order to give Hank a hand," Mike explained. "To bridge the gap between the technology and the biology, there were several details about how the molecules talked to each other, and how they transmitted impulses. I studied cytology, histology and biomedical engineering – in my spare time (he added when the General stared to look uneasy). Well, I got hooked on the medical sciences. So I spoke with the School of Medicine.

Since then I have been doing one course after another on my own. My reputation was enough – that's my academic rep, not the other one." he added when Rob Gauthier snickered. "It was enough to convince them that I could do most of the work independently.

"Once a month, I met with members of the faculty and reviewed what I'd learned. I wrote the exams with the other med students. Whenever I could, I attended rounds in the various disciplines. That didn't hurt my standing either, when I could hold my own with the best of the other medical students. In the end, I was very successful. The University already knew that I was unable to attend graduation for security reasons. And no, I didn't tell them about the black-suit guys. So I received this yesterday in the mail." Mike presented Dr. Gauthier with a manila envelope. Rob Gauthier had already guessed what was in it, so when he withdrew the medical degree he was not surprised.

"I still need to do a residency." Mike said. "We have a much better hospital here than on the Alameda base. I figure that I could do it here, on my free time."

"What were you thinking of doing it in?" the doctor asked.

"Trauma surgery and battlefield medicine, though, I realize that the second part might have to be done in the simulator lab, but we have that facility here, Alameda doesn't," Mike answered.

The General was stunned. "I'm not sure how to take this," he said. "Are you going to be a doctor or a researcher?"

"Both," Mike replied. "That way I can't get stale at either, and the base gets a 'two-fer'."

In the end Mike was given the ok for the residency, and after a two week vacation, at an undisclosed Caribbean island location, Mike opened the SCORCH files for the first time since his dad's murder.

In the back of his mind, he recognized an ulterior motive for wanting to complete his father's work. Yes, he wanted to protect America's troops in action, but he also wanted to stick it to the black-suit guys. If he handed a working force field over to Uncle Sam, then his father's legacy would be complete and their attempts will forever have failed. That thought drove him to dive into his research with an impassioned vigor.

If he was passionate about his research, Mike was equally so when it came to his residency. He happily put in eight to ten hours in his lab each day, followed by the same amount of time in the base hospital. People began to wonder when he ever got the chance to sleep. The only thing that suffered for the two years that it took him to complete his father's work was his incessant womanizing. The female population of Kennedy Air Base started to think that he had taken a vow of chastity, and as they knew that he was nominally Roman Catholic, they began to wonder. Then, two years to the day that he began the project, Captain Mike Colford called and asked General Urnbreach to join him in his lab.

As they were virtually alone in that section of the

facility, he addressed the General informally. "You're gonna love it, Unc!" he announced. He took a hand gun from a locked cabinet next to his work bench. He threw a switch. Then a second later, Mike said, "Watch that meter, Unc," and as the General looked in the indicated direction Mike yelled, "Fire in the hole," and discharged the weapon in the general direction of the work bench.

The blast of the gun was followed immediately by the sound of a bullet falling on the table top. At the same moment, the general saw the needle on the indicated meter jump slightly. "Do you know what you just saw?" Mike asked.

The General looked at him smiling broadly, "Had I been looking in the right direction I am sure that I would have seen the working prototype of our new force field."

"You were looking in the right direction," Mike told him. "You saw the needle move?" Urnbreach nodded. "Now examine the bullet," Mike directed.

General went over to the table and made to pick up the slug from Mike's gun, but hesitated. "It's ok," Mike said. "It's perfectly cool." The General picked it up. As Mike had said, it was cool to the touch. It should have still been hot or at least warm. And... "It's not at all damaged!" the General said with surprise.

"That's right." Mike answered, "That movement on the meter that you observed was measuring the energy that the force field drained from the bullet, not just its momentum, but also from its heat. It isn't damaged, because the field stopped its motion by absorbing all of its kinetic energy, while at the same time absorbing the radiant energy. This field doesn't use brute force to stop projectiles, it stops them by draining them of all their energy, and, as you observed, it also absorbs that energy. In doing that, it replenishes the energy it expends stopping the projectile. The conversion isn't perfect. The energy it drains doesn't totally recharge its reserves. Though it comes close, and it should work equally well on energy weapons, should Alameda ever finish their research."

"Actually, your timing is really very good," Urnbreach told him. I received word from my friends at the Pentagon that Alameda conducted a successful test this week. It is still preliminary, but it is very promising. They may catch up to you very soon."

Mike thought about that for a moment, and then he smiled. "Dad would be pleased that we finished the defense before they finished the weapon. The one thing he often said was that he hated the fact that he had to create ways to defend against ever more vicious weaponry already designed by somebody else." He looked upward and added, "For you, Dad!"

Three months later, Dr. Michael Colford, MD, FACS officially received his licence to practice medicine. It was just coincidental that, on that same day, he was promoted to the rank of Major at the ripe old age of twenty-three. It was that move that alerted the men and women in the black suits. Only, it was too late. As Mike had surmised, there was nothing more they could hope to gain from him. The official powers-that-be had his father's force field, and Mike, himself, was on too many radars for them to try and take any vengeful action against him.

With the pressures of his research done, Mike settled into his medical practice, though still tinkering on small projects for the Defense Department, on the side. Just so long as they were defensive projects. He found that he really enjoyed being a doctor. In medicine, he had really found his niche. He was helping people. Although he missed the intellectual challenge of his father's research, Mike found another use for the time that he had devoted to completing it.

Since that first night with Jerri Linton in the storage shed behind Hanger C, Mike had learned a lot about meeting women. At a time when the rest of the world was practicing sexual responsibility and working to develop emotionally stable relationships, Mike Colford had become, in his godfather's words, "the last great Lothario". He was just careful enough not to run afoul of any of the Air Force's regulations on fraternization, all the while gaining a reputation around the base that rivalled even his reputation in university.

Then, just as Mike's life was getting comfortable, serious trouble erupted in New York City. Ever since the early 21st Century, groups of disaffected young people had been moving into the New York City area, first squatting in abandoned buildings on the fringes of the city's industrial areas and outlying boroughs. It had been a nuisance that the authorities tolerated until a large group banded together taking a much more aggressive stance. In the summer of 2070, a number of these more militant groups descended on Manhattan. They overran Central Park and invaded some of the buildings on the Park's western border. They erected barricades and fortified the buildings. They took their residents hostage and began publically executing them, one at a time, until the city brought them food and other non-lethal supplies.

In the days that followed, the militants moved out from their strongholds at irregular intervals. When least expected they executed raids on offices in the financial district taking prisoners they felt they could ransom. They looted from the offices for whatever they could use. Often, they killed the security guards outright and took their weapons. It was only the measures that had been put in place following the terrorist actions in the very early years of the century that prevented them from storming the Wall Street exchange itself. It wasn't long before their actions attracted other militant groups and ne'er-do-wells from the surrounding cities who swelled their ranks. In a few short weeks, midtown Manhattan degenerated into a bloody war zone. The ferocity of the militants was unforeseen and unprecedented. When New York's finest were very rapidly out gunned and overwhelmed, Governor Corman called in the National Guard.

Even the first Guard units were taken by surprise by the ferocity of the militants' attacks. They were overrun and disarmed. Some Guardsmen, mostly officers, were immediately executed. The survivors were added to the number of hostages being held. Their weapons and equipment were taken by their captors. A short, fierce, all-out war in the heart of Manhattan, ensued. The casualties were enormous. The gangs gave a new definition to the word "brutal". Casualties and hostage shootings grew beyond all reason. The casualty levels had passed way beyond local health care systems' ability to handle. That's when the Guard's commander turned to Army and Air Force to get much-needed medical help. The regular forces responded with mobile trauma units to treat both the combatant and civilian casualties. Mike was among the first of those regular forces to be sent to the conflict zone.

As the commander of a forward MASH, Major Colford was appalled at the brutality of the aggressors. They showed little regard for the age, gender or station of the people that they maimed or killed. Mike and his team were treating young people, old people, children and even babies. The casualties ranged from Wall Street tycoons to the homeless who were still trying to sleep in the park at night. They treated the priests, ministers, rabbis and civic leaders who had tried to negotiate with the militants. The attackers took medics and nurses who tried to aid the fallen, as their prisoners. No one was immune to their violence.

Ultimately, the Guard was forced to meet the militants' aggression with equal ferocity. As the fighting reached its fiercest, Mike and his team were working round the clock for days on end. In his forward position, he saw injured from both sides, though most often they were the civilians who had gotten caught in the cross-fire. During their sorties the militants began using the local residents as human shields, but when as the number of casualties among the guardsmen and civilians mounted yet again, the guardsmen were forced to go right through their "shields" to take out the aggressors. Despite all efforts by the Guardsmen to minimize the injuries, they escalated beyond anything anyone ever expected.

Repeated seventy-two hour sessions in a makeshift OR set up in the hotel on the south side of the Park left Mike and his staff drained. They fought almost as hard against their own depression as they did to the save lives of their patients. The nightmare lasted six very long weeks. Over three thousand civilians and fifteen hundred National Guardsmen were either killed or injured. Of the two thousand militants that had taken over the park and its environs only a few hundred remained. In the end, the militants fought like berserkers, and like berserkers they fell, taking so many innocents with them.

The battle zone was virtually destroyed. In the final hours of the conflict, the militants set the captured apartments Central Park West from 64th to 72nd ablaze. All that remained of the Historical Society building was a pile of bricks and cinders. Most of the Park had been devastated. Almost all of the buildings on its grounds were destroyed. The water in the Jaqueline Kennedy Onassis reservoir was completely fouled. Most of the trees and shrubs in the Park were reduced to ash. The Lake and The Pond were pools of sludge.

The authorities, at all levels of government, estimated that the rebuilding and restoration could take almost a decade. Figuring out a solution to the problems that gave rise to the conflagration in the first place would take at least as long. If anything at all came out of the conflict, it was that community leaders finally agreed that there was a real problem, and at last an imperative to try and address the issues emerged. In the aftermath, Mike finally found an answer to the question of what he would do with his father's estate.

He had long since separated his legitimate inheritance from the money that the black-suit guys had used to try and frame his father. The "dirty money", as he called it, had been put into an investment fund and was growing ever larger. The fund managers were extremely talented, very aggressive and incredibly innovative in their strategies. Since Mike really didn't want the money, he allowed them to play the riskiest parts of the markets. In the ten and a half years since the day that Mike activated the SCORCH protocol, the fund had grown to almost a hundred million dollars.

Immediately following what the press and the politicians called the "Victory in Central Park", a multi-million dollar fund called the "Park Survivors Fund" was quietly and anonymously established by Mike, to aid the civilian victims and help the families of the fallen men and women of the Guard.

Of that "dirty money", Mike held back ten million dollars, the original amount put into his father's bank by the black-suit guys. He announced publically that it would go to establish the "Dr. Michael Kelly Memorial Fund". This fund was to help the families of the fallen and incarcerated militants. In the aftermath of the fighting, no one seemed to remember that their wives and girlfriends, children and parents were victims, too. Fortunately, many religious groups, of all faiths and denominations, agreed with Mike and were inspired to contribute to the Kelly Fund, when most others were still ruled by their anger and refused to help. In a plush office in Washington, the move was not lost on the man with the yin and yang tattoos. Mike would have been very pleased to learn how much his fund had galled his father's murderer.

Always up for a challenge, when in 2071 the call went out for a replacement physician for the new International Space Station, one who could speak both English and Ukrainian, Mike jumped at the challenge. After a crash course in treating patients in space, and the usual intensive astronaut training with the International Aeronautics and Space Agency, (NASA's successor), Colonel Mike Colford found himself heading to the space station for a six month assignment in space. His official mission was to conduct a broad spectrum of research projects while serving as the station's Chief Medical Officer. Mike also made arrangements with Yale's School of Medicine to do research into the possibility of performing certain types of surgery in space. That study was inconclusive, but Mike returned to earth with one more reason for the women to swoon. Now he was Dr. Mike Colford, astronaut.

A week after his return, Mike was visiting with his "uncles" on base. Over a drink at Dr. Gauthier's house he regaled then with stories from space. At one point, in between stories, his "uncle" Jim commented, "That was a gutsy move you made, Mike, but don't think that I don't know why you sought that space assignment."

"Whatever do you mean, Unc?" Mike asked feigning innocence.

"I know that you think that you run things around here, son, but you do know who's really at the top," Urnbreach said. "I see all official communications, and I know that the boys in Alameda have been pushing the Pentagon to assign you to their project. And then there's General Gowan, who wants to get you to fly for him in the Canal Zone. Gowan remembers you from when he was a flight instructor here. He figures you can be a doctor by day and combat pilot by night."

"Well, Alameda is actually the one that I was really

trying to avoid, I confess. They are forever trying to build a better particle weapon," Mike answered. "Everyone in this room knows that Gowan is never going to force me to fly combat missions, I'm a physician. There is just no way that I am going to bomb suspected drug labs from Mexico to Columbia. The only reason that their governments don't care about the number of false hits the coalition planes make is because it's usually the poor people that they hit, and nobody cares about them."

"Except you?" Rob Gauthier offered.

"Don't kid yourself, son," the General said. "We care; but our intelligence is so bad, mostly because the cartels are brutal in the way that they handle would-be informants. No one dares speak up, so more often than not, we're shooting blind. The cartels will kill half a village to get back at one informant, and not lose a moment's sleep. More than that, even if we get lucky and we take out a lab here or there, another replaces it in a nearby town or village, before the smoke has even cleared.

"We're always playing catch-up ball. The way they operate, the cartels must have money to burn. Look, their equipment and ordinance is often right up there with ours. Just between us, I think that they are getting help from some well-placed people here in the States and overseas. I just wish I could figure out what anyone here would be getting out of it."

"You mean apart from money, Jim?" Rob asked. "The only reason that the cartels haven't given up and retired like the rest of their lot overseas is because now the folks down south have taken over the overseas markets. Our war on terror overseas also broke the backs of the Asian cartels more than fifteen years ago. That opened the door for the southern drug lords to move in on their territory and swallow up their operations. As long as the drug money doesn't fund terrorism or interfere with their rule, many Middle Eastern governments ignore them. Now these cartels have more money than God. They've swallowed up the Mexican gangs and control real estate as far south as the Argentina's northern border. They are as much into territory now as they are into money. They control most of the governments in Central and South America."

"I suppose you're right, Rob, but it galls me. It doesn't matter who is supplying them, that's an international force down there. Everybody's sons and daughters are getting killed, not just Americans."

"If people love money more than their own sisters and brothers, Unc, they'll sell out their own family, let alone country," Mike said sadly.

The General took another long drink and said, "I hate to say this, Mike, but I almost wish that you would take that new tech of yours down there. Maybe we could bring an end to this." Everyone fell silent for a few moments and then the General added despondently, "Who am I kidding. The stuffed shirts in DC still haven't authorized funds for its wide deployment yet. 'It's too expensive to refit all of our fighter jets' they say. 'The power units for the troop vests cost too much.' It never changes: Dollars before soldiers – that's the worst side of the powers-that-be." He fell silent again. Suddenly, the night had taken on a darker mood.

The General did brighten up a moment later to add, "I shouldn't tell you this, but what the heck, your clearance is high enough. The word is that the F-165's from Lockheed-MacD are being designed with your tech in them, Mike. They'll have the new pulse cannons from Alameda, too. There may be hope yet."

The next major event in Mike's life came about two years later, when 'Project Symphony' was announced. It was an adventure that Mike couldn't pass up. But not everyone in Mike's life was happy about that...

"Just another two kilometers," Dr. Gauthier called from his console.

"Another two klicks!" Mike's whole body groaned. Already slumping, he was sure that he would fall over on the treadmill any second. Then the doctor's nurse walked in; the pretty, young one in the tight jumper. Mike tried to recall her name. It was...Gillian, Gillian Green. From somewhere deep inside Mike found that "little bit extra" to straighten himself up and firm up his stride.

Approaching the doctor's console, carrying Mike's chart, she gasped in unfeigned astonishment,

"That's amazing! Colonel Colford. I've never seen anyone do fifteen kilometers at that rate – and still going strong." That tinge of admiration in her voice was what kept Mike from wavering until she had left the room again. The moment the door closed behind her, he hit the manual override and stopped the machine. He slumped to the tread, at first gulping air by reflex, then, as reflex gave way to training, Mike quickly brought his breathing under control.

"You bastard!" he gasped at his godfather, as soon as he had the breath to speak. "You fiddled with my console read-out. 'A quick five klicks; keep it at seven KPH' you said, 'An easy run,' you said. What'd you do? Set my monitor on the treadmill to read only a third? Was I running at more than twenty kilometers per for almost forty minutes?"

"And that's something to complain about?" Dr. Gauthier retorted. "Fifty years ago only a select few had the ability to achieve that speed, and sustaining it for even a fraction of that time was unheard of."

"Fifty years ago I wouldn't have had to do it either," Mike complained, "My doctor wouldn't have been a maniacal slave driver."

"And," the doctor countered, "fifty years ago I wouldn't have had to be, because you wouldn't be training to go on some cockeyed mission to the 'Twilight Zone'."

"What's that, another reference drawn from your passion for 20th Century television?" Mike adopted a more reasonable tone. "Uncle Rob, you're missing the whole point. You know that, all over the world, scientists have been working seriously with the theory of alternate dimensions since the late twenty teens. Only now, it's not just a theory. We know that other planes of existence are real. Now we know that matter can pass from one resonance plane to another, living matter. We want to know, we need to know, what's going on in our neighbouring universes."

"But to risk someone of your genius", the doctor pleaded. "Mike, I've known you all your life. I did your enlistment physical. At sixteen we had it all figured out – how you were going to use the Air Force to keep the black-suit guys away, and get the education that you lost out on in that damned College Lottery. Back then this "Mr. Volunteer" thing was your way of keeping yourself out of combat duty and in school, at the military's expense. So after earning more degrees than I have, including your MD, you've reached the point where the brass wouldn't dare risk your ass by ordering you onto such a hair-brained project. So what do you do? You volunteer!"

Mike shook his head, "Not exactly true, Uncle Rob. You remember what Uncle Jim said? They still want me in Alameda. I'm a doctor, Unc, I don't make weapons. It's not my fault if they can't get it right on the first try. Dad had the right idea, 'build a defense in case someone else builds the weapon.' That same tech, that he conceived and together he and I perfected, can also be used on space craft for missions beyond the solar system. It's the answer to the problem of micro-meteorites. Even more, if the meteorite problem is as great as the theorists think, the shields could also be an auxiliary power source."

"You spend so much time on the wards or in your lab that you haven't been keeping up on the general reports, Mike. Alameda already turned in a functioning and reliable bug-free upgrade to their particle beam weapon. It's confirmed, the weapons are being installed in the F-165's, just like the General said. You're off the hook. You don't have to go anywhere."

"Ultimately though, Uncle Rob, that doesn't change a thing," Mike said, just as his "uncle" believed that he had won his point. "You said it yourself just a moment ago. I joined the Air Force to learn! More than anything, that was why I joined the Project.

"I am going to have the opportunity to journey to another universe. If I could continue with the Space Program for another two hundred years, the chance that I would see another earth-type planet is virtually non-existent. In a few weeks, I will set foot on another Earth. Who knows what I'll find when I get there."

"My point exactly!" Dr. Gauthier countered. "No one has been able to discern what dangers might await you," the older man added, almost pleadingly. "We send cameras of all sorts to other dimensions. They all come back with corrupt data, something to do with the shift process. All we have been able to ascertain about this new world of yours is that you can survive over there – at least you can if you're a small animal." He added the latter because small animals were the only test subjects that they had been able to experiment with.

Finally, when it was obvious that the doctor still wasn't going to win this long-standing argument he added in a seemingly defeated tone.

"Well... anyhow, your 'wedding date' is set for next Tuesday... To Max," he quickly added when Mike nearly jumped out of his skin.

"We're doing the interface implants on Tuesday morning. Hell, with your atavistic tendency to chase anything even remotely female, a computer is probably the only spouse that would have you!"

"There, you see," Mike retorted, "I don't spend all my time working. And considering the fact that one of the links is going into my hypothalamic-pituitary axis, Max will have a definite edge on insuring my fidelity."

"We don't know for sure, yet, whether he will have much, if any, control over your endocrine secretions or neurotransmitters. Even if he does, it is only supposed to be for stimulating your adrenalin systems or enhancing your sensory abilities, should you need the help."

"We shall see, won't we?" Mike quipped as he reached for his shirt. "But, while I'm still 'single', tell me, do I have time to shower and change before Nurse Green goes off duty?"

Dr. Gauthier's groaned, "...And you're our first representative to other dimensions?! – *LORD HAVE MERCY!!!!*"

If Mike had ever thought that his "uncle", General Urnbreach, could be a problem, he was not alone. While he was taking his physical, over at the Control Complex of Project Symphony the General was treating Maureen Sims, the project's chief systems designer, to a little of his idea of 'military efficiency'.

"Doctor, all I'm saying is that you seem to be wasting a lot of valuable time on these 'resonance energy displacement' tests. You have all the energy you need. Isn't that why we built you your own cold fusion generator?"

The General was beginning to get to her, again, but Maureen kept her cool. She knew it would bug him if he couldn't get a rise out of her, almost as much as his pushing bothered her. "*It's a shame he's so thick sometimes,*" she thought, "*apart from that, he is one hell of a guy, even if he is old enough to be my dad.*" Quietly she answered, "General, it's not how much power we are using, but the kind of harmonic field that that level of power will generate. Within the control complex we are protected, but Dr. Craig is not too sure about the area immediately surrounding this building. The amount of power that he anticipates we'll need may set up a harmonic wave that could be harmful to the local environment."

"What? Is this some ecology thing? You're worried about Dr. Gauthier's petunias or something?"

"Not exactly, look, as the Chief Systems Engineer I'm just running the simulations that Dr. Craig asked me to run. You should be asking him about that, and he is out at the moment."

To his misfortune, that was the moment Mitchell Craig happened to return. General "Ironbritches", as Mitch liked to call him when he wasn't around, rounded on him before he had even seated himself at the console.

"Well, Craig, how 'bout it? What's with these extra tests?" he demanded.

Mitch drew a deep breath, '*Stay calm,*' he told himself,

'He can't get to you if you don't let him.'

"It's like this General," Mitch began calmly, "We've never sent a living being of human size through the gate before. You see, both Mike's size and complexity make a great deal of difference. The resonance shifter scans the organism to be shifted, measuring the specific density, overall cellular resonance and a host of other factors, at the cellular level, for each organ in the living body. It then feeds the data to Max, and Max computes the proper resonance field and shift frequency for each separate part, and then 'he' assembles them into a resonance pattern that will shift the animal, or in this case, the person, into the desired dimension. It is not unlike composing a symphony, except in this symphony all the notes are played at once."

"So, what's the problem?"

"As I said, we have never shifted anything as big as a man before. You know the problem that we've had sneaking the smaller animals past the animal rights watchdogs dogging our gates. They have spies everywhere, and you know what they could do to us in Washington if they wanted to cause trouble. The last thing we need now is a Senate committee investigating us. Such a thing could set us back a year, at least."

"OK, that I can accept, but I still don't see the problem," Urnbreach barked.

"*He's not a physicist,*" Mitch kept reminding himself. "It is a question of harmonics," he explained as patiently as possible. "Just as a sound wave can set up a sympathetic vibration in an object that it strikes, the dimensional shift field would cause a harmonic disturbance in everything around it, if we didn't have a damping field surrounding the shift chamber.

This damping field creates the containment field that dissipates the resonance wave as it strikes. The problem is that we can't dampen the resonance field any more than we already do without interfering with its effect. So, to protect the Control Complex, we developed a means of dissipating the greater part of resonance field harmlessly into the outside environment. At least we believe it's harmless. That's what we're testing now."

"You mean you're not sure?" the General asked, a little more subdued.

"It's just that with a subject of human size and complexity going through the dimensional gate, we aren't sure that a few trans-dimensional harmonics might not be created, outside of our control."

"I see," the General became pensive. "And this could be dangerous to our base personnel?"

"No, probably not" you see, General, the wave has to be very specific to affect living organisms, as their energy patterns are constantly in flux at the cellular and even molecular level. What it could do is set up transfer harmonics in the materiel of the base itself."

"But you're not sure?"

"No Sir, that's why we're running the simulations," Craig answered, cautiously. Knowing the General, he was afraid of what was coming.

"Well, cut them short," he ordered. "Otherwise you might get your Senate committee investigation anyway, in front of the worst possible body, the *Budget Committee*."

The warm evening breeze and the scent of the young woman's perfume drove far from Mike's mind all thoughts of General Urnbreach, his impending "union" with Max the AI, and anything else associated with Project Symphony. His only reminder of the ordeal of Robert Gauthier's examination was the romantic evening he was sharing with the good doctor's nurse, Gillian. It didn't seem to matter to her that Mike had a wicked reputation as a skirt chaser, anachronism though it now was, in the late 21st Century. To use a very old word, he was *smooth*, at least that's how he saw himself.

Mike felt that he could charm almost any woman into believing whatever he told her. He was one of the last of a dying breed in this era of emotional honesty and responsibility. He had ruffled a lot of feathers here and there, but when a woman was with him, Mike really did have the knack of making her forget all his "bad press" in the pleasure of the moment.

Of course, it also helped to have his other reputation. There were still a very large number of women who would say "yes" to a date with a living legend. More than one had thought she was the one who could change his ways overnight, and jumped at the chance to try. What had surprised Mike was that Gillian didn't seem to be one of those.

Mike's evaluation of the evening was that everything

was going perfectly. The dinner at *Chez Maurice* was, as expected, perfect. The dancing at *La Palacia* was heaven – naturally. And then, a moonlight stroll along the beach, as a prelude to the night cap at his beach-front condo, with the quiet music, the longing looks and bedroom eyes – "*Never fails,*" Mike thought. "*Someone ought to pass a law – make a man have to get a license to do that.*"

But, in the wee hours of the morning, as Mike lay awake beside Gillian, her boss's words came back to him. "Who but a computer...," (though Max was already far more than just a computer) would have an old skirt-chaser like him? He looked down at the young woman sleeping beside him. Had she really dated him, or just his image? Had she made love with Mike Colford or was she "sleeping with" Colonel Colford, the astronaut-doctor, soon-to-be dimensional traveller?

This line of reflection puzzled him. What was it about this young woman that had caused him to question himself like that, or had the questions always been there only to have Gillian bring them to the fore? Either way, why were they important to him that night? Just then, she stirred slightly and the sheet slid down to expose part of her lithe young form, and the moment passed. Mike snuggled close to her. "*Better get some sleep,*" he thought, "*tomorrow's another day and Gillian's not due at work till ten.*"

As it happened, it was Gillian who woke first, as the warmth of the first rays of dawn shone through the half closed bedroom curtains.

"*Good thing that window looks out onto the beach.*" she

thought. Not that Gillian was shy, but there were some things that she felt were not for general viewing. For a while, she lay there, with her head on Mike's chest feeling its rhythmic rise and fall, his warm breath in her hair, inhaling the scent of his body. It was not where she expected to be.

She couldn't believe it at first, when he asked her out. "The Mike Colford" wanted to take her out to dinner. Though as the dinner progressed, and she had to wade through all that bull he was feeding her along with the fine dinner, it began to look as if his reputation was as bad as she had heard. She couldn't understand why so many of the girls on the base had been swept off their feet by this guy. How he ever earned his reputation was beyond her.

Having met the Colonel at the office several times before, Gillian had found it hard to believe the negative stories that she had heard about his various conquests were really true. He was always so warm and engaging, not to mention kind. Then she sat through his dinner chat. How could anyone be attracted to that garbage? In the cab on the way to La Palacia, she had just about decided to dump him at the first opportunity when some instinct stopped her. As she tried to reconcile the Mike Colford she already knew with the jerk with whom she had just eaten, some cracks in his "Casanova" veneer began to show. She began to wonder if there was something that he didn't want her to see, that Mike was hiding behind all the trivial nonsense of his dinner conversation.

Though at first it was just an attempt to take control of the conversation, to get beyond the triviality that had dominated the table talk, Gillian began, in subtle ways, to explore the man behind the line, asking Mike things about himself that, until then, he wasn't volunteering.

She asked about his childhood. Mike told her of his mother's death, when he was just three. Her father was Irish, though he died when she was young. She was raised mostly by her Ukrainian mother. Mike explained. "That was why when I was six years old I decided to learn to speak Ukrainian, to honour mom's memory."

Mike was expansive when he talked of his relationship with his father, and how they worked on projects together. He positively glowed when he talked about building the simulator with him, and how he first learned to fly at the age of nine. When she asked if his dad was still alive, Mike said almost nothing. Only that he had died just before Mike joined the Air Force. She noted the shadow that crossed his face when she asked the question and didn't press further.

He then turned the conversation onto his friendship with Phil. He said that he owed Phil and Phil's family a debt he didn't know if he could ever repay. Again, he didn't explain what the debt was or, why he owed them. He smiled, both inwardly, and outwardly as he talked of his relationship with Phil. He recounted some of Phil's stories about his rabbinical studies, but she didn't understand why it was, that Mike said he was not able to attend Phil's ordination. It was clear that it was something that saddened him a great deal.

When Gillian asked about his career he was evasive when it came to his earlier work. He only said that he completed his father's research before concentrating almost completely on Medicine. He touched briefly upon New York, but tried not to put a downer on the evening by telling her of its horrors.

As they walked on the beach, the conversation turned to space. When it came to the space program Mike spoke very poetically of the view from the space station. He regaled Gillian with amusing anecdotes, many of which heaped high praise on his comrades aboard the space station, even at his own expense.

As the 'cracks' grew, letting Gillian have a look at the man she believed to be underneath, she liked what she saw. She liked it a great deal. The real Mike Colford was really the great guy that she thought that he was. His "Casanova" routine didn't jive with the real man at all, in fact by the end of the evening there didn't seem to be any doubt as to where she would be spending that night. Staying with Mike just felt like the right thing to do.

Gillian lay there, remembering, letting the memory warm her like the morning sun on her back. She didn't want to move in case she somehow lost that warmth in the reality of the morning after. So, for a long moment she remained there, until she was sure that Mike was not about to wake up right away. Then, softly, she slipped out of bed.

She decided against taking a shower, *"I'm sure it's more pleasant with two..."* she told herself. Instead, she elected to do that part of her regular morning routine that could be done anywhere.

"You don't have to be at home to do your stretches and breathing", she told herself. She glanced at her clothing on the chair. That dress would definitely not do for stretches, not that nudity had ever stopped her from exercising at home. It was just that in someone else's home, you never knew who might walk in. Glancing around the room she found Mike's shirt where it had fallen by the door. It would do fine. Gillian snatched it up as she headed for the living room, pausing to smell his scent on the garment once more, before slipping it on.

It was fully 07:00 when Mike finally woke to find himself alone in bed. The place next to him was empty and cool. That, and the aroma of coffee on the warmer, told him that Gillian had been up and about for a little while. He smiled to himself. Though Mike really liked to wake up with the woman he'd just slept with, there was also something to be said for a morning work-out after a cup of freshly brewed coffee, particularly the kind of work-out he had in mind.

He pulled on a pair of shorts and padded towards the kitchen. He found the coffee on the warmer, but no Gillian. He stuck his head back into the living room, not believing that he could have passed her without noticing, particularly since he had not failed to note that all of her clothes were still draped over the chair in the bedroom (a fact that had helped him to wake up in a hurry).

Mike reasoned that Gillian must be in the bathroom. As he passed through the living room, less distracted by what he expected to find, a chance glance, out of the corner of his eye, found her. Gillian was sitting in front of the plants that adorned the patio entrance, absolutely motionless, with her back to the morning sun that was streaming in through the French doors. Her serenity was radiantly profound. Framed in the sunlight Gillian seemed to glow.

The scene confused Mike. It aroused in him the desire to go to her, hold her and make love with her as he had never done with any woman before, and it also held him back. He couldn't bring himself to disturb the scene. Mike had a sense that this moment was extremely important to Gillian, and he couldn't bring himself to interrupt her bliss. So he stood there, transfixed, both by what he saw and by his reaction to it, a most novel reaction for him. Silently he observed her, until he could no longer endure the, as yet unanswered, call of nature.

When he emerged from the bathroom, Gillian was no longer there. He could hear her humming softly to herself in the kitchen. Though the moment seemed lost, its effect stayed with Mike, continuing to puzzle him.

Mike slipped quietly into the kitchen, approaching Gillian from behind, softly wrapping his arms around her. He was so quiet and gentle that she didn't even jump. She just leaned back into his embrace. Neither spoke right away.

"Earlier riser," Mike commented, breaking the pause, "missed you when I woke up."

"I didn't want to wake you. You seemed so peaceful. Besides, I like to do my morning meditation at dawn. The whole world seems so fresh and new at that hour. It leads so naturally into the silence."

"Meditation, huh", Mike commented, "like 'TM'?"

"Sorta, we call it 'Hebrew Meditation', it's a form of

prayer that goes back to the earliest forms of Judaism."

"So you're the religious type?" Mike asked.

Gillian dangled the "Star of David" that she wore on a chain around her neck, "This aint just jewelry," she said.

"You do that every morning?"

"Mornings, on my lunch break, and in the evening just after work."

"Funny," Mike said, "last night I wouldn't have pegged you as actively religious."

Gillian disengaged herself from Mike's embrace and turned towards him so that she could look him straight in the eye. "Last night was not something planned." she told him. "I don't end all my dates in someone's bedroom. I don't know how to explain it, there is just something about you that touched me."

Mike did a mental double take. A part of him was ready to do handsprings, the rest of him was scared witless. This sounded serious. It was time to change the subject. It was obvious that his plans for their early morning activities might best be abandoned. His mind raced to find a graceful 'exit'. Without realizing it, Mike stammered nervously.

"Uh.. Um.. How about I fix us some breakfast while you grab a shower, that is, if you want one.... I've got to do my daily work out at the gym, I usually shower afterward," he extemporized.

Gillian smiled, to mask the sinking feeling that suddenly hit her. She nodded her assent. As she headed for the shower, she couldn't escape the feeling that he was backing away from her. What had she said? "*Well,*" she thought, with just a hint of mischief, "*at least we'll show him what he'll be missing.*" As she approached his bedroom door, Gillian slipped out of Mike's shirt and holding it in one hand, turned back towards him.

"Your hamper's in the bathroom?" she asked, innocently. Mike could only nod, meekly, and Gillian smiled to herself, playfully, as she turned back towards the bedroom, holding the image of Mike's expression in her mind. She hadn't yet realized how hurt she was really feeling.

When Gillian emerged from the shower, Mike was already dressed in sweats, as if he really was heading for the gym after breakfast. It made her feel a little better. For a little while longer, she could convince herself that maybe what Mike had said was true, that he really wasn't pulling back. That thought and a little small talk got her through breakfast and the drive back to her place. When he dropped her off, Mike kissed her with passion promising to call her again, soon. Gillian could almost ignore that little ring of insincerity that was in his voice, at least, that is, until she arrived at the office later that morning. Waiting there, for her was a bouquet of roses – what had come to be known as the traditional 'Colford kiss-off'. It carried a card full of sweet sounding words and seemingly earnest promises, but she knew better. More than once, she had seen a friend get the same flowers and card.

Gillian emerged from the washroom some time later,

her eyes red and puffy. Mike, she had decided, was obviously not the man she had taken him for the night before; she must have been taken in after all. Only, why did it still hurt so much? This was more than just the sting of someone who had been taken in by a smooth operator. The rest of her day went by very slowly.

After he dropped Gillian off, Mike actually did go to the gym. Normally, he went on his lunch hour, but after lying to Gillian that morning, he felt that he should at least go through the motions of his daily work out. That lie really bothered him for some reason. In fact, this whole thing with Gillian Green worried him greatly. Instinctively, he ran for cover. The first thing he did upon arriving at the athletic complex was to call his florist and order a dozen –"...no two dozen roses....Yes, the usual card," Mike heard himself saying. Even though, deep down, he wanted to say no, he wanted to say something special, to apologize for being a jerk. He just couldn't admit to himself that he had been – that he was– scared silly by what he was feeling. He certainly wasn't ready to tell Gillian, not yet. So he let his reflex take over, managing, in one phone call, to make matters immeasurably worse. Though he knew it would, he did it anyway, hating himself for doing it, and not knowing why.

And so went the rest of the week and the weekend. Several times each day, Mike felt compelled to pick up the phone and call Gillian. Each time, he resisted the impulse. For Gillian, the week was no better. First she was depressed, then she became angry, but mostly, she was puzzled. Could she really have fallen so completely for a guy who was such a jerk, and on their first date? Thinking about the exchange concerning her star, she wondered at whether he might be anti-Semitic, so she asked her boss.

"Not possible!" Dr. Rob assured her. "His best friend, Phil, is a Rabbi. He always speaks very highly of him. He says that he helped him escape after his father was murdered. I'm sure that it isn't that." That left Gillian even more confused. She struggled to reconcile the man she saw that evening, with the man she woke up with the next morning. The memory of that night filled her with pain and longing. She wished with all her heart to see that Mike Colford again.

When Monday came, little seemed to have changed for either of them, but as Mike checked into the base hospital, for his implant surgery the next day, he found that the battle between his desire to call and his reflex not to, raged stronger than ever. Going to sleep that night and waking up the next morning, Gillian was foremost in his thoughts. But, by then, he felt that it was too late; that he had missed the moment. "She'd probably think that it was pre-op jitters", he told himself, but was it?

Tuesday morning was just another work day for Gillian. That's what she told herself. It would be an easy one, too. Because even though Dr. Gauthier wasn't a neurosurgeon, he was going to be on hand for Mike's – *"that is Colonel Colford's"* – surgery. It was just another day, yet the morning dragged on to the point where the clock seemed to have all but stopped. Gillian found it harder and harder to concentrate on her work. By noon, she surrendered, and picked up the phone to call post-op to see if he was out of surgery yet. He wasn't. Gillian skipped lunch that day instead she went to the observation gallery in the Med Centre's surgical wing. "Just to see…"

And Tuesday morning was anything but normal, or easy, for the team over in the Project's control centre. Maureen Sims and her team spent the morning glued to terminal screens and going over the reams of continual output that Max was generating as the link-up between the AI and Mike was in progress. Tracing the logic of an AI that advanced is difficult at the best of times, but today, it was impossible. By the time the implants were complete and 'functioning', the experts had thrown up their hands in defeat.

"We'll just have to wait for Colonel Colford," she told General Urnbreach. "We need Mike to confirm the functionality of the links".

"Are you telling me that you and your team of whiz kids can't tell whether that piece of trillion dollar hardware is functioning properly or not?" The General was not pleased.

But Maureen stood her ground, "It's like we told you from the beginning, General, there are no guarantees that all of the circuits will interface with the neural pathways in Colonel Colford's brain; and if we start experimenting on our own, before Mike is ready, we could do some serious damage, perhaps even kill him without meaning to. Besides, Max wouldn't let us, even if we tried. All AI's are programmed with the heuristics and algorithms necessary for ethical development. To date, Max appears to have developed them with maximum efficiency."

"Great, now we have the machine telling us what to do.

And just how long will it be before Max will allow us to begin testing the interface?" The general's tone was its most condescending. Maureen had already given up counting to ten as a way to avoid giving him the response he deserved. Instead, she would look for an excuse, any excuse to change the direction of these seemingly useless discussions over matters that couldn't be helped anyway. Just as she was about to change the subject, one of the members of her team did it for her as he called out excitedly, "They're talking!"

Sure enough, when she and the general went to check, the readouts that signified communication between Mike Colford's verbal and auditory processing areas and Max's "Special Communications Port" were active. The mood sobered, though only a little, when Max refused to divulge the content of their conversation. "It would be unethical," he explained. "It is after all a private conversation."

Soon afterwards, everyone was busy again. Screen after screen, register after register began to show signs of renewed activity. There were several sections of Max's processing units that had previously been inactive, but now were a flurry of activity, and as far as anyone could tell, everything was functioning according to design. Maureen glanced over at the general, as he moved from station to station in the control complex. Each time he received a new report, he smiled. He has a nice smile she thought, if only he would use it more often. Just then her master console bleeped bringing her thoughts back to her work.

With the interface complete, Project Symphony really took off. The following weeks flew by as Mike and Max tested their new links, looking for the best pathways, the cleanest signals. Wherever possible, they tested the limits of Max's control over Mike's autonomic systems. But they could only go so far, Max refused to try altering any of his endocrine levels, or fiddle with any of his hormonal or endorphin systems. "The risk to you is too great," he insisted, "Some things will just have to wait until it is necessary before we know if I can affect those areas or not."

As a physician, Mike had to agree with him, but both the scientist and the adventurer in him would rather have tried. In any event, the rapid pace that they kept, advanced the project considerably. Mike had very little time for anything other than the Project. If there were no setbacks the plan now was to go with the earliest projected shift date.

The night before the shift, Mike was again required to stay in the base hospital, for observation. This close to Dr. Gauthier's office, he found that his thoughts were more about Gillian than what was coming up the next day. As he lay in bed, unable to sleep, he realized that in the past weeks he had, by necessity, put her out of his thoughts, while he attended to duty, or so he thought. Now, he found that he was feeling very guilty for not making time to call her, at least, to say 'hello', maybe tell her that he was still thinking about her.

"*You're right, you should have.*"

The sound of Max's 'voice' in his head made Mike jump. The link between them was a lot more complete than anyone had expected. Max could actually hear Mike's thoughts. At the same time, Mike had virtual access to Max's memory banks, and could get the AI to process the most complex of problems for him just by thinking about them However there were times when the closeness of the link disturbed him. Rob Gauthier's marriage analogy didn't cover it by half.

"You have had her in the back of your mind for at least as long the interface has been active, Colonel", Max went on, *"and if my comprehension of your memory paths is correct, for even longer. Query: Is this what humans call 'love'?"*

The use of that word frightened Mike, and the idea that it did, bothered him more. Max's sensors told him that this was an unsettling topic at the moment. He calculated that it was best to leave the subject for a later time. He said something to Mike that sounded vaguely like an apology and suggested that if Mike was having trouble sleeping that he could increase the levels of serotonin in his anterior reticular formation and allow him to get some sleep. Mike wasn't really paying much attention as he mumbled his assent, he was feeling very confused by the major question Max had proposed. *'Is this what humans call love?'*

Abruptly, Mike was asleep. If he had been able to realize what Max had done, it would have been pleasing to know that an important facet of the interface had finally been tested and had worked perfectly. He would have been somewhat less pleased however, if he had known that the soft knock at the door that Max had innocently kept from waking him, was Gillian, especially, had he known how long she had stood on the other side of that door working up the courage.

Gillian knocked a second time, then quietly opened the

door a crack. Seeing that Mike was sound asleep, she crept over to the bed and kissed him softly on the cheek.

Though Mike was asleep, Max definitely was not, but he had lowered the potentials in the neural interface so as not to disturb Mike with his own internal processes. So Max was unaware of Gillian's presence in the room until her lips touched Mike's cheek. This form of sensory input was foreign to the AI. He carefully accessed Mike's memory cells to find out what it was; a difficult task to perform without waking up his human partner. It meant that Max had to probe very slowly and quietly through Mike's neural pathways so as not to raise the level of cortical stimulation to the point of consciousness. For an instant, he was drawn back to Mike's somata-sensory area, when his sensors detected a small drop of moisture landing on Mike's cheek. By the time he had collected enough data to deduce what had transpired, his sensors registered the sound of the door closing behind Gillian. For the rest of the night Max ran and re-ran his ethical programs, weighing the facts and trying to decide whether to tell Mike of what had taken place while he slept.

The next morning, the level of activity in the control centre was frenetic when Mike arrived. He didn't think it could get much worse, but as his departure time drew closer things, reached and passed the fever pitch. There were no obvious nerves. There were just so many things that could not be left to chance, and had to be verified and re-verified and then verified again.

At the centre of the activity, Mike was hard at work; far from a naive observer. He had had an active role in the design of many of the systems, including most of those that now formed his link with Max.

Many of the final tests, now being run, were last minute checks of his new hardware and interfaces. 'Zero hour' was set for precisely noon and, with Max's help they were on schedule almost to the second. At five minutes to the hour Mike stepped onto the platform in the centre of the resonance chamber as the final calibrations were verified. For an eternity, first Maureen, then Mitch checked out the key systems and sub-systems of the human-AI interface, which was Mike's only way of getting back in the event of an emergency. All the while, the General stood watching, seemingly stone-faced.

At first, Mike took the expression on his face to be one of impatience, as one test followed another, and as each system check meant yet another system check. As the clock ticked down that assumption seemed less and less accurate as the General, himself, ordered certain systems double checked, and then checked yet again. As the thirty second count began, it occurred to Mike that his "uncle" was worried about him. Today, Urnbreach was more than a commander sending one of his people into a potentially hazardous situation. He was concerned for his "nephew". Mike was touched by the realization. He was only half aware of the final count, until he heard Maureen reach five. And when he looked up again, the last image that he saw was Gillian Green standing in the doorway. It was obvious that she had been crying. Then everything was a blur.

Mitch Craig gave Max the instruction to initiate the shift. Mike's whole body seemed to whine. For a moment, he couldn't hear Max in the background, answering queries from Mitch. Just as he thought he was going to black out, the whine stopped.

"I've arrived." he thought, half out loud, *"But where."*

"It looks like a below-ground or semi-basement structure," Max offered. *"Right!"* Mike thought, remembering that he had to curb less-than-necessary rhetorical questions if he didn't want Max to answer all of them. *"but where?...".*

"Data insufficient," came the brief reply in his head, reminding Mike that his alter-ego was a computer, the most sophisticated ever built, but still a computer. Until Max added, *"Any guesses?"* That sounded almost like Mike.

Mike took stock of his surroundings. He was in a large rectangular room with walls, floor and ceiling of concrete (or maybe even plascrete?). It looked very much like a holding cell in some twentieth century prison, only larger. In one of the long walls a large steel door was set with a smaller door inset, filling the wall opposite were four other doors, about half the vertical size of the large one. There were only two small lights lit at the top of the walls, at either 'end' of the room.

In the dim light, Mike made a closer inspection of the large door and its smaller sub-section; both were secure. What he found inset in the walls on either side of the large door confirmed his notion that this was a holding facility. As he ran his hand along the wall, he found a catch that released at his touch. A small sanitary unit folded out from the wall. *"So much for human dignity,"* he said to himself.

Still without the aid of extra light, he followed the wall around to the series of doors on the opposite side. He could have used the powerful mini-light in his kit, but when he first approached the wall, he noticed a few other devices, black boxes that he couldn't recognize. Just in case they were cameras, he didn't want to alert an observer, who might have been only half-watching, a supposedly empty room, to his presence. Mike was sure that if he missed something Max, would pick it up with his image enhancers. It was only then, that he realized he was able to see clearly, Max was enhancing his visual acuity.

"Sorry, I was expecting you to request it..." Max explained in response to Mike's unasked question. *"...Shall we continue?"*

By the time they had checked out the first three doors, Mike was beginning to feel as if his first trip was going to be a very short one. There was no way he could get out of the cell, without returning to the shift chamber.

"Or using explosives" he joked to himself, as he assured himself that the fourth door was as secure as the three previous. He had just enough time to realize that Max had not responded literally to his quip when the small segment in the large steel door on the opposite side swung open. Two, rather large, uniformed men stood framed in it.

"See," one said, "I tol' ya the motion sensors registered a straggler."

He pressed a stud on his belt and the door beside Mike silently slipped upward. He was about to say something when the second man raised his hand, pointing at what looked like an old fashion TV remote control at one of the black boxes. As the door behind him slid open, the black box flashed, and a force of some kind catapulted Mike through the door landing him on his behind in the bowl of an arena.

It took only a second for Mike's eyes to adjust to the bright sunlight, but he was already aware that he was not anywhere that he wanted to be as cheers, jeers and catcalls accompanied his appearance. Getting quickly to his feet he observed a knot of people huddled together in the centre of the oval. Many wore a look of sheer terror, and all of them were staring intently at the far end of the field.

At that end, were two more doors. As the doors began to open Mike thought that he could hear the roar of lions or tigers. Images of ancient Roman spectacles flashed through his head as Mike sprinted over to the group. As he approached, one young man turned towards him, startled by his presence.

"You're not one of us," he managed to say, immediately turning his attention back to the far end of the bowl. "You weren't with us in the holding area or group confinement."

"New arrival," was all Mike answered, his eyes now also trained on the far end of the field. Big cats, lions and tigers had emerged from the doors. For the moment they stood there, clawing at the air.

"Why aren't they attacking?" he thought out loud.

The young man turned back to him again, a look of amazement on his face.

"You're definitely a new comer," he told Mike. "Everyone knows that the guards hold them back with a force field; to get them good and worked up. They can see us and smell us, but they can't get at us; not for at least five minutes, anyway."

"And after that?" Mike asked, sure that he would not like the answer.

"Not sure," was the reply, "For obvious reasons, our kind never attend as spectators, but I hear that after the five minutes are up an automatic mechanism selectively opens sections of the force wall at random. The crowd can tell where, by using those special glasses." He indicated the green eyewear sported by most of the crowd. Mike had taken them to be the current fashion in sunglasses.

"If the opening is by one or more animals the carnage begins. The reason for that selectivity is to get us all worked up."

"And it works pretty damn good," Mike thought as he began to smell the fear around him. He realized that Max must be enhancing his senses. He also began to feel the effect of a controlled adrenaline release.

"You must be stimulating a little nor-epi, too," he said to Max, *"I don't feel frazzled in the least."*

"That's good," Max replied, *"But don't you think that your weapon might prove useful now?"* he inquired.

Then Mike remembered the 12 mm automatic in the

special concealed pocket inside his jacket. The General had ordered it. Mike had been adamantly opposed to carrying arms. "It was a gun that killed my father." he reminded Urnbreach, as if that was necessary. The General's argument was firm, "Look, Mike, I know what guns mean to you, but this is a very special case. You are going on a very dangerous mission into possibly hostile territory. You need to be prepared. My first impulse was to order you take an M-24 along with you, but they are large, and rather offensive looking if you should happen to arrive in the middle of a group of sweet little old ladies. The 12 mil, for its size, has the stopping power of an old 30-06. You can hide it in a pocket, and it should get you out of almost any situation, short of a full scale attack."

A young man close to him noticed the weapon. "What the hell is that?" the young man asked.

In spite of their rising terror, others turned to look as well, as they became aware of what was going on.

It surprised Mike that so many people didn't know what a gun was, but instead of answering, he asked a question of his own.

"That force field, does it go both ways?"

"Unlikely," an older man answered, "that would take a lot more energy than necessary. They only want to keep the cats away for the moment and we're sure as heck not going to rush into it, leastwise, not usually."

"That's what I thought," Mike answered as he raised the weapon. He took aim at a large cat, at one end of the pack, as far from the pen doors as possible. He fired once. The older man's assumption was correct as the bullet drilled into the poor beast's head, the hollow point slug causing its skull to explode. Automatically, the other cats reacted. Already frenzied from the scent of human fear that was on the wind, those closest to the slain animal reacted instinctively to the smell of its blood. They pounced savagely. Mike fired again, killing another animal at the opposite extremity. Again, its closest neighbors pounced on their dying companion. Some tore the animal to pieces while others fought them for a share.

Initially, the spectators were stunned. To Mike's amazement, it was as if no one here had ever seen a gun before. Even the guards on the walls were taken aback, and for a moment they didn't react. But Mike did.

"This way," he shouted to the intended victims of the spectacle. Roused from their own shock by his call, the group followed.

Twice more, Mike fired through the force screen into the pack of frenzied animals. What he was up to was immediately evident to those with him. As the pack fell upon the slain animals, a path opened up right down its centre. If Mike was right, they should be able to pass right through the large hole that he had created. If that luck held, there would be a shot at freedom on the other side of the animal pen.

Then, with freedom so close, it was almost denied them. At first, the guards positioned along the walls, had been as stunned as the audience. Never before had anything like this ever happened and, to a man, they were caught napping.

Mike and his group were just at the force screen, within a few feet of the open cat pens, when one of the guards came alive enough to radio the control centre. As silently as the doors of the holding cell, the doors to the pens began to slide closed. But what had been a knot of terrified victims only moments ago, had now come alive, too.

A very large man stepped from the centre of the group, threw his shoulder up against the bottom of the door and heaved. Its progress was slightly slowed, but the door continued to close. It looked as if Mike's valiant effort would be for naught, when the old Colford luck kicked in, and Mike found out why his gun was such a novelty.

Up on the wall, the guards had roused themselves and were all firing at the man who was trying to force the door. Instead of bullets, the crackle of energy beams sizzled in Mike's ears. Mike had just enough time to make a somewhat startling realization as a wild shot from above missed its intended target and hit the door track, spot welding the door in place. Then Mike Colford turned and did something he thought he would never do. He fired his gun at another human being.

He fired four shots, and four men fell into the arena, just as someone in the control centre overrode the automatic systems and dropped the force barrier holding back the frenzied animals. Freed of the restraint they pounced, not on the fleeing prisoners, but on the fallen guards, as Mike hurried the last of the prisoners through the open door to the animal pen. The attacking beasts drew the fire from the remaining guards who were desperately trying to save their injured comrades.

Once through the door, Mike dashed across the pen to the gate on the other side. As he had hoped, there was no lock. Big cats rarely try to break jail, especially on their way to the dining room. A simple latch stood between them and liberty, and in a moment, they were in the corridor. On the wall, there were signs, in Latin, pointing the way to the receiving dock. Expecting to be overrun with guards at any moment, Mike kept the group moving as fast as he could.

Their luck held. They encountered no guards before reaching the receiving area. The guard on duty was more than willing to open up for them, even without a demonstration of Mike's hand weapon; what they found on the dock explained the rest. There were several vehicles out there, but none of them had wheels. They were all hyper-magnetic hover craft powered from a central source.

"Great?" he said, "No doubt they can turn them off at any moment, and track them with ease too, I'll bet."

"I'm afraid so," his young friend confirmed.

"Then we run," he announced flatly. "At least they may not expect us to try to make a break for it on foot," he added when several people looked at him skeptically.

Well, he had gotten them this far, everyone thought, so when Mike started to jog towards an obvious exit they fell in behind.

Within moments, they crossed the loading dock and were about to make a break when Mike, who was still in the lead, ran into – Nothing - The hardest nothing that he had ever run into. The force of his forward momentum encountering the unseen barrier knocked him backward. Mike landed unceremonious on his behind. Two of the younger members of the group, who were close behind him, helped him up. "I was afraid of that," his curly haired friend announced. "The guard at the door didn't resist because he knew that the force fields were already in place."

"We're not caught yet," Mike told him flatly. "There has to be an emergency exit somewhere nearby – it's a public building." That his reasoning might not hold in this continuum didn't occur to Mike right away. But, as luck would have it, he was right. A few seconds of searching was all that was needed to locate a panic door on the other side of the loading dock. Mike's elation lasted only long enough to reach the door. The box attached to the top of the frame told the story.

Mike hit the panic bar and nothing happened. He no longer expected anything. He recognized the box for what it was: A magnetic security lock. Unless the fire systems were triggered at the central security console, that door would be held closed with up to five thousand foot pounds of force. Short of starting a major fire on the loading dock, there was nothing he could do – or was there?

"How are those hover things run?" he asked, of no one in particular, indicating the hover craft that were 'parked' in the loading dock area.

"Magnetic fields, generated by superconductors in the base," he was told, "powered from the central power station."

"Do they have any internal power?"

"Rechargeable emergency batteries, but they only have enough juice to get a craft down safely in the event of a central black out."

Mike answered, his hope renewed. "Can one be brought over here?"

"I'll get one, if possible," another man said, heading off towards the craft.

He was back in a few seconds in a craft that Mike was sure was most likely used for the local delivery of small packages.

"OK," he asked, "how is it charged?"

The old man opened the front cowling, revealing a length of cable with a heavy duty male plug on one end. "It plugs into a standard socket, like that one by the door, there." He indicated a female receptacle by the door.

"That's what I thought it was for." Mike said to Max.

Pulling a screw driver from his emergency pack, Mike set to work on the far end of the power cord, and soon had it free of the vehicle. Next, he wedged the power cord's connectors into the seams on either sides of the magnetic door lock. From the cab of the hover truck he took the floor mat. It was rubber, just as he expected. He wrapped it around the plug end.

"Stand back," he ordered, and shoved the male plug

into the charging receptacle. Instantly the magnetic lock exploded into a shower of sparks. At the same time all the lights went out in the loading dock. Obviously, Mike had shorted out a main system somewhere.

Still, within seconds, the emergency power kicked in and with it came the wail of fire alarms.

Mike cursed. "If they weren't sure where we were before, they know for sure now," he said. "Everyone come on." He hit the door harder than necessary, it gave without resistance.

As he passed through the door, Mike heard a low whine near the dock; undoubtedly, a power vehicle cycling. They were on them. Determined not to give up, Mike ran down the side of the building in a direction away from the sound of the hover craft. He turned the corner and stopped dead. There in front of him was, what at that moment he considered to be the most beautiful site he had ever seen. It was big, blue, with four wheels and the words "US AIR FORCE" stenciled on its side. He didn't know how it got there, but he was overjoyed to see it.

The whine of the engine was getting louder now, their pursuers were in motion. Mike called to his group to follow him and ran for the bus. For once, he appreciated not only Sgt. O'Malley's mechanical genius, but also his habit of forgetting the keys in the vehicles' ignitions. It saved Mike the time necessary to hot wire the bus.

His fellow escapees at first were a little startled by the noise as the engine turned over, but, by now, they were ready to follow Mike anywhere.

Mike threw the bus into gear and took off with a lurch just as the first hover vehicle came into view.

"Hey, Curly," he called to his new young friend.

"Aaron," the young man corrected him.

Mike nodded in acknowledgment, "Mike," he replied, continuing, "How fast can those hover-things go?"

"The official cars, like that one behind us, are quite fast. They draw their power from the Security grid. They aren't hampered by the load on the main traffic grid," Aaron told him, with a worried frown. "Most of 'em can reach speeds as high as 35 or 40 kilometers per hour."

"Oh really?" Mike's grin was so broad, it was infectious and Aaron found himself grinning in spite of his worry. An instant later he found out why, as Mike put his foot to the floor. The needle on the speedometer rapidly climbed to 70 miles per hour leaving the pursuit craft far behind.

Mike's elation at apparently out running his pursuers was short lived. As soon as they were clear of the arena, he made a series of quick turns whenever he came to something resembling an intersection in hopes of foiling any attempt by their pursuers to figure out their course, or radio ahead for a road block. What really began to worry Mike was that he actually wasn't driving on a road at all. All the traffic used the magnetic suspension ways above. Not knowing the real purpose of the concrete channel he was using suggested the possibility that he might just suddenly run out of road. Abruptly, as if thinking about something made it so, Mike turned a corner and found himself in a blind alley. The alley ran for about fifty feet and ended in a concrete yard with a large door in the opposite wall. Mike hit the brakes hard and shifted into reverse. He would have to back track and find another way out.

As he put his foot onto the accelerator, he heard an unmistakable sound: a police siren. He braked again and looked at Aaron, who turned towards an older man close by.

"Sam?"

"There is probably an all-points alert out for us," Sam asserted. "It is unlikely that they know we have made it this far so quickly. From the echo, it sounds like they're doing a pattern search."

"But they'll see us if I back up," Mike said. "And any passing car can see us anywhere in that yard ahead." To the whole bus he said, "If anyone has any ideas, now is the time. Even if they aren't coming directly, they will be here very soon."

"There is one possibility." It was the big man who had tried to stop the door in the arena. "These channels we have been following are service paths. The slave crews are marched along here so that the people above don't have to see us in the main thoroughfares above. Those doors lead to the underground tunnels containing the power lines and transformers for the transport system, as well as the sewer system, and other basic services. The guards used to tell us to turn our backs while their Group Leader inputs the code for the door. No one ever considered that I'm tall enough to see the Group Leader's reflection in the helmet of the guard that is standing in front of me as he inputs the code. After being assigned to city maintenance often enough, I think I know how the number is constructed."

"If that's all we've got..," Mike said.

Aaron and Sam were forced to agree with him.

The big man, Gabriel, and Aaron left the bus and went to the door directly ahead. As they walked, Gabriel explained.

"The code is actually made up of two parts. A standard prefix, and a suffix based on the district coding along with the particular door you are entering." He lifted the cover plate on the number pad. "Half of the suffix is right here." He pointed to a serial number on the inside of the cover. "If I am right, that is the number that goes between it and the prefix," he said, pointing at a two digit number just below the curb above.

"And if you're wrong?"

"I'm not sure. It may just happen that the door won't open, or, if there is a high security nexus at this location, it will get very noisy and very crowded around here, very fast."

Gabriel input the last series of numbers, then paused before pressing the "OPEN" button. He looked over at Aaron nervously and gesturing with his thumb towards the bus asked, "You don't suppose that that contraption can fly too, do you?"

Aaron shook his head. Gabe took a deep breath and

punched the button. Nothing happened. The light below the pad still glowed red. Everyone on the bus saw it, too. A general feeling of panic began to build as the sound of sirens came closer.

"What now?" Gabe asked.

"I don't know." Aaron answered honestly, "Maybe our new friend has another magic trick up his sleeve. Right now, I am drawing a blank–" Aaron stopped dead in his tracks, as if his own words had been a revelation to him.

"Of course!" he practically yelled. Gabe turned to look at him in surprise. "That's it!"

"What is?"

"A blank."

Gabe looked at him without comprehension. "What is?"

"A blank." Aaron repeated. "Didn't you tell me that you worked on systems in the north end of the city?"

Gabe nodded, still not understanding.

"I have been up that way several times. All of the curb numbers in that area have three digits. Here they have only two. We need to put in a blank – or more precisely– a zero. C'mon, try it again."

The sirens were almost on top of them now, as Gabriel entered the revised code, adding the zero before the street number. They held their breaths as he hit the OPEN button again. Swiftly and silently the door slid upward. The two men exhaled in unison, and Aaron waved the bus forward. As soon as it was inside, Gabe hit the close button on the interior panel.

As the door closed, interior lights came on. At that same moment the sound of sirens passed overhead. Mike killed the engine and joined them by the door. To Mike's surprise only Sam followed.

"Won't your first attempt to open the door register on a console somewhere?" he asked.

"Not likely," Gabe answered. "The regular work-crew guards make mistakes all the time. As far as I know, at least, only the high security areas, those with security nodes inside, are alarmed at all."

"They don't think that we could possibly know their coding system," Aaron added.

"To be honest," Gabe added, "If it wasn't for their spit n' polish, we probably wouldn't."

"What do you recommend now?" Mike asked.

"It all depends," Gabriel answered. "What is your machine's power source?"

"It's a diesel." Mike said, figuring that was a sufficient answer.

"A what?"

"A diesel engine," Mike could tell that he still drew a blank. "An internal combustion engine," he added. The other three still didn't seem to understand. "This could take a bit of explaining," he said.

"Just tell me this..." Gabe asked, "...does it require sunlight, or the city power grid to operate?"

"Neither."

"Then I recommend that we keep going," he said. "These ..." he pointed at a set of diagrams on the wall,"...are maps of the tunnel systems. All tunnels are all at least as wide and as high as this. If your machine has the range, we can get from here to the city's edge," he indicated the area on the map's border, "without having to go above ground. And if we exit by this gate…" he indicated a point on the map "…we follow the service grill used for the sewage treatment system as far as the woods. From there, we can go as far as your vehicle can take us."

"What if we run into work crews?" Mike asked.

"On Saturn's day!?" Aaron scoffed, "Not very likely. You know the Patricians are very 'religious' about their recreation. Even the slave handlers and guards must have their weekend."

So it was settled. Gabriel took a moment to re-check the diagram on the wall, the four boarded the bus, and they were underway once more.

As predicted, the route was without incident from then

on. Even stopping periodically, so Gabe could consult the floor plans, they made good time, soon enough they would be out of the city. Still, as they drove there was an air of caution throughout the bus. There was no idle conversation. Apart from receiving directions from Gabriel, Mike was alone with his thoughts. He had time to marvel at the day's events so far.

He found himself with a great many mysteries. Although the weaponry of the arena guards, and the transport vehicles, suggested a technically advanced society, the architecture that he had seen above was much like that of his own dimension's twentieth century. Although very ornate, to the point of classical art, the construction materials used were only conventional brick and concrete, no plascrete, crysteel or any other translux metals. Then there was Aaron's reference to "Saturn's day", in his own world the ancient Roman name had long since been shortened to "Saturday" – and there were the Roman style spectacles in the Arena. Only these were Jews being thrown to the lions not Christians – and this society still practiced slavery! None of this made sense. It was as if the Roman Empire still existed in the 20th Century.

Mike followed Gabriel's directions for about two hours. Finally, they reached the exit door he was looking for. Again, Gabriel and Aaron held their breath as they activated the security lock until the door began to lift, and the bus drove out into the early dusk.

Once free of the city, Mike drove flat out along a service grill. All around him was a desert of scrub grass and dust. It was common practice, Aaron informed him, for the Security Police to scorch the ground for several miles around the cities, to make escapees easier to follow. Mike made no comment, but continued to drive in silent amazement at the lengths to which this regime was willing to go in order to maintain control.

After a time, Mike began to relax. It was very likely that the security police had not even considered the possibility that they had made it out of the city.

"You're probably right," Max agreed.

Mike almost jumped. It had been so long since his AI partner had said anything, that he had, for the moment, almost forgotten him.

"Some 'husband' you are!" Max responded. Mike jumped again. Max just made a joke!

"I don't understand it myself," the AI responded, *"I seem to be growing in a manner not consistent with my design."*

"It would seem so," Mike responded with a touch of sarcasm. *"Who knows, it may actually be a good thing. What do your ongoing diagnostics say?"*

"All systems are functioning normally," he responded in a more computer-like tone, adding, *"There's not much that we can do about it now, so best advice is: 'Don't sweat it', I'll keep you up-to-date if there are any changes."*

"You sound more and more like me," Mike replied.

"Aren't we a pair?" Max quipped. Mike stifled a laugh. He didn't want to have to explain Max to his new friends just

yet.

As they moved farther away from the city, the mood on the bus relaxed a little and low keyed conversations started up among the passengers. Mike took the opportunity to ask Aaron about the arena spectacle that he had landed in the middle of.

"Bread and Circuses," Aaron explained. "The New Romans want to keep the masses entertained to keep their minds off the pressing issues of the day, so they provide spectacles in the arena. Some weekends there are gladiators, on others, it's animals fighting animals. Many weekends, they also have criminal executions. Those can get very gruesome. It's meant to send a message to would-be criminals or rebels. I hear that last weekend they coated a group of Christian zealots with pitch and set them on fire, of course, the crowds loved it. Then, every so often, if they feel that the slave population is getting too large to manage, they choose a random group of slaves and feed them to the lions, or pit them against the gladiators. Sometimes we're the human torches. To the crowds it's all just a big show."

Mike was aghast. "That's barbaric! How do they get away with it?"

"The masses eat it up." Aaron told him matter-of-factly. "It has been this way since the time of old Rome."

After that, Mike continued to drive in silence; unable to get his head around the depravity of it all. He had been travelling along the service grill for about an hour and twenty-five minutes when a stand of trees came into view and the ground started to rise. As the ground began to slope upward to the left, the grill that Mike was using for a road, turned off to the right and he had to continue the journey travelling cross country staying close the tree cover to prevent a chance discovery by a random patrol. At one point, following Aaron's directions, he turned into the trees.

As the trees closed in around them, Mike located a dried river bed that was heading in the right direction; though he had to slow to a crawl to navigate the rougher terrain, he was able to follow the stream's bed for a good distance. After Aaron's caution about random patrols, Mike was becoming concerned that, by now, the Security Police would have begun searching for them beyond the city limits. While the dark bus was not readily visible through the trees, there was the possibility that their pursuers would locate them using infrared sensors. He shared his concern with Aaron, Sam and Gabe.

"I've never heard of such a device," Sam told him. "How would it work?"

"It would home in on a heat source, like the heat of our engine," Mike answered.

"But all our vehicles, short and long range, operate on super cooled engines, infrared detection would be useless in tracking them."

"And a super cooled engine, like their own might actually mask the body heat of the craft's occupants. You're right, it would probably be worthless," Mike finished.

'That's a break,' he thought, *"but let's be careful anyway,"* he added to himself.

"Amen!" Max added.

After about two hours of zigging and zagging in and out of the trees, Mike brought the bus to a halt. "Sorry folks," he announced, "this vehicle wasn't made for this kind of terrain. We'll have to go on foot from here."

"That's OK," Sam told him, "where we're going isn't far very from here anyway. Besides, this machine of yours is a wonder as it is, son. Who would have thought of a vehicle that runs on rubber disks and has an engine that runs hot?!" And he filed off the bus following the others, shaking his head in amazement.

Mike just sat there. He was equally, if not more, astonished. A world with energy weapons, and magnetic hovercraft with superconductor engines, but they had never seen a handgun or a diesel engine before.

"You had better get a move on or they'll be out of sight," Max reminded him, bringing Mike back to 'reality'. He grabbed the keys from the ignition and began to trot after the group who were already a fair distance along a well-concealed path (A path that Mike surmised likely had a lot of false turns in it), but he was in excellent condition, and caught up to the group with little exertion.

Sam's "not far" turned out to be almost a two hour hike. Everyone was glad when Aaron, who was leading the way, made one final turn stopping abruptly at an apparent dead end. He reached through a mass of vines and pulled on something. Very slowly the lichen covered rock face, in front of them, slid inward and the group filed through the portal. Mike was still near the end of the group, having been collared by two women who he discovered had been this world's equivalent of physicists "before" (whatever that meant). They wanted to know all about this "internal combustion engine" and had bombarded him with so many questions that he had no chance to ask any of his own. Now as they entered, a man, armed with a large blade stopped him.

"You're not one of our people," he challenged, but Aaron, who had been waiting for him just inside the door, stepped up.

"He may not be, but he was in the arena with us, and he was the one who got us out. Pass him on my responsibility," he directed. Silently, the guard stood aside.

"Sorry about that," Aaron apologized, but the big man with the blade still eyed Mike with suspicion. When Mike just shrugged it off, Aaron continued, smiling, "C'mon, I'll introduce you to our community."

They crossed the small entrance chamber and followed a narrow passage that terminated in a much larger natural cavern out of which Mike could see several more openings into other chambers. It was apparent that most of those openings were of human construction.

The larger cavern that they entered was now filling with people and the group of escapees was welcomed by relatives and friends as though they had returned from the dead, which wasn't far from the truth. Mike then noticed Sam. He seemed to be looking for someone, worriedly. Then the worry left his face as a voice cried out.

"Father, Father, over here."

Sam turned in the direction of the voice, his face at once aglow. Mike turned too, in shock. He had recognized the voice. There, rushing towards Sam, was Gillian Green. It was impossible, but there she was.

"It's not her," Max informed him, *"Gillian's been in the shift chamber control room all day – 'Just in case Dr. Gauthier needs something.'"*

"But that's her, too," Mike argued, watching as the young woman hugged her father tightly. *"Could it be that parallel a universe?"*

The next few minutes were, for Mike, very surreal. After what seemed to him an eternity, Sam disengaged himself from his daughter and turned to face him.

"Michael," he said, very formally, "I would like to present to you my daughter, Jillian Greenstein." Then, to Jillian, he said "This is the man who is responsible for saving our lives. His name is Michael, uh, hmm..." Sam faltered as he realized that he didn't know Mike's last name.

As if on cue, roused himself and extended a hand towards her, "Mike Colford", he said, and then stopped, not sure how to continue though not yet aware that he was staring very intently at the girl.

Jillian took the extended hand, but instead of shaking it she gently pulled him forward and kissed him on the cheek.

"Thank you for bringing my father back to me," she

said earnestly, "…and my friends call me 'Jill'," she added.

Mike felt himself blushing without knowing why. Before him stood the woman who had so occupied his thoughts over the past while; and yet it wasn't her, but her exact double - right down to her name. She was so similar to the Gillian he had left behind, yet the girl in front of him was a stranger.

In a day of firsts, here was yet another, Mike Colford was struck dumb in front of a woman. But the moment didn't last as several of the people, he had rescued from the arena, converged on him with various relatives and friends who wanted to meet him. Among them, Mike was certain, were members of the community's leaders. These welcomed him warmly, and earnestly. They shook his hand, some even hugged him tightly – they smiled and thanked him, and then stood back and observed as he was greeted as a hero by the other members of the community.

Almost immediately afterward, the new arrivals were ushered off to a meal in another large chamber, just off the main one. There was no noticeable announcement of the meal. Shortly after their arrival, while Mike was still meeting people and shaking hands, the entire group moved, as one, into the adjoining cavern. This one, Mike noticed, was not a natural cave. It had been hewn from the rock.

Supper, for that's what it was, was simple, nourishing, and rather tasty. There was ample without surplus. No one took more than needed and all plates were cleaned. Afterward, the clean-up was equally efficient. It was followed by a period of informal recreation, during which, Mike was again collared by Molly and Ruth, the two physicists who had occupied him so effectively on the trail. This time, they had with them, two or three others, apparently scientists, as well, by the nature of their questions, who managed to occupy his time until the next time the community began to move as a group.

At the same time, as Mike was being welcomed as hero, back at home, in the Control Centre's Administrative Conference Room, a meeting was in progress that felt, to most of those present, as if it might go on forever. Senator Jansen Reall, chair of the Project Symphony oversight committee, was leaning on the project scientists and General Urnbreach to move the project to its backup location.

"...We were just lucky that nothing too 'Top Secret' winked out of here this time," he argued, "...and you have no idea of how much of the missing base will return with Colonel Colford do you? Assuming, that is, Dr. Craig, that you can retrieve him."

"We can bring him home..," Mitch replied, already straining to keep his voice level. Tempers, all around, were beginning to fray. It was amazing how this guy could find anyone's sore spot and then just grind away at it. "...And in response to your last question, we are working on that right now. Max should be able to predict which, presently missing pieces of the base, are tied to Mike and will return with him. Others would probably return with him from other vibrational planes, as he returns from those particular voyages.

"You're assuming that there'll be other 'voyages'," Reall

cut in.

"...As to any danger their return might pose;" Mitch continued, without acknowledging the interruption, "...we anticipate that the various buildings and hardware will return to their original places..."

"...If they do return..," the Senator anticipated. Mitch ignored him.

"What are the problems involved in moving the project to the backup control site?" the General asked, hoping to seem the voice of reason and calm. "Doctors, couldn't you continue to run the project from here, for the moment. Download Max's data-to-date to the twin AI at Pine Falls and then do a quick switch over of control? Dr. Simms?"

Maureen took her time in answering, and when she did, there was an uncertainty in her voice: "It may not be that easy, and I'm almost positive that the twin AI could not do the job Max is doing."

"Is there a problem with the other system that we should know about?" the Senator asked.

"No..."

"Then why can't you transfer control?" Reall demanded.

"It's Max...."

"He is malfunctioning?" Reall cut in.

"No...."

"Then what?" Reall was shouting now.

"Let the gal finish a sentence, Jan," Urnbreach said with that quiet firmness that no one, so far, ever dared to ignore.

"Thank you, General," Simms said, feeling the moisture trickle down her back. Reall, who was hovering predator-like over Maureen, looked at the General for an instant and then retook his seat, momentarily cowed, but still smoldering.

"It's like this," she began, "the longer they are in operation, the more common it is for most AI's, artificial intelligences that is, to develop their own algorithms for handling complex problems such as for priority of processing; forms of response; when they might ask for further data, and a host of other things. It's analogous to though, obviously, not exactly the same as personality, and we actually do refer to it as 'artificial personality' or 'AP'. The AI's of Max's generation have a tendency to develop an AP much faster than any previous machine. They obviously pay attention to how different people refer to them, or talk about them. Eventually, they choose for themselves the name they 'like'. As you may be aware, one's name is fundamental to a person's sense of self. It is the same for AI's. The name 'Max' was what Colonel Colford always called him. Even before the interface there was a strong affinity between the two of them."

"So far that doesn't seem to me to make much difference," Reall cut in, "the AI at Twin Pines has been active just as long and has all the same background..."

"Jan!" the General barked, the anger evident in his voice. Then to Maureen, "Please continue, doctor."

"Thank you, General," she responded, genuinely surprised at his defense and his deference. "You see, it's no longer that simple. The neural implant that was inserted into Mike Colford's brain was originally only meant to be an emergency device. It would have allowed us to monitor his body functions with greater accuracy than regular telemetry, including, in theory, a link directly into his speech centres. The hope was to be able to maintain verbal communication with Colonel Colford without using any overt transmitting devices, particularly since the usual type of voice transmitter has proven very unreliable across the dimensional plane. Also, special connections into the anterior reticular formation were designed to facilitate the release of certain hormones, endorphins, and neurotransmitters in emergency situations. What we actually achieved, however, was unimaginably greater than anything we had expected.

"We got our first surprise while running the initial tests. The verbal link worked, perfectly. The hormonal and neurotransmitter release simulations were also successful. The big shock, however, was the level of communication that existed between Colonel Colford and Max. Through the connection in the reticular formation, Max seems to be connected to virtually every part of Mike's brain. He can almost, perhaps actually – we're not sure – read Mike's thoughts; certainly those the Colonel voices internally. That was an advantage that we had not counted upon."

"Big fuckin' deal!" Reall seethed, sarcastically. Maureen didn't rise to the bait, though she was developing a fantasy about a neurological procedure that she would like to see performed on the Senator.

"It was a big deal. When the colonel shifted," she continued, "...all hell broke loose. I immediately ordered a complete systems check to see if a glitch, in any of the control systems, might have been responsible for the harmonic effect. One of the first areas we checked was, naturally, the AI. The standard hardware tests were all negative, until we checked his core capacity. As you may know, an AI's core contains its entire active memory capacity. The only secondary storage involved is the system backup. As such, one would expect the core memory to be used up very slowly. Our readouts indicated that Max had used more than a quarter of his core memory. A unit that should have had enough memory for two hundred years, had passed the one quarter capacity level in moments.

"We immediately began to run a level one diagnostic on the supposed free portion of Max's systems. He rejected it. His exact response was, 'Not now, Dr. Sims, Colonel Colford needs my fullest attention at the moment, my apologies'".

"So you have a polite computer, I'm impressed," Reall sneered.

"But that's not the proper form of response, idiot!" Urnbreach hollered at Reall, as if he were a raw recruit, "If you'd open your ears and close your mouth, you might just learn something. And if you can't, then just plain *SHUT UP*! I haven't heard the final word on this and *I* want to know."

"Well, the final word is pretty unbelievable. You see, Max is no longer an AI."

At that remark even Reall began to listen more intently.

"Although he is still, technically, a machine, Max has definitely become a living, sentient entity."

Reall was immediately on his feet, about to pounce, at least figuratively if not literally, upon Maureen Simms – until he was brought up short by the rather imposing presence of the General rising to counter his attack. The senator stood there, hovering, for the briefest moment, and then shrank back into his chair.

With an apologetic nod to Maureen General Urnbreach reseated himself, keeping one eye on Reall.

As soon as Urnbreach had retaken his seat, Dr. Gauthier took up the narrative.

"As near as we could figure, it happened during the shift – this was later confirmed by Max. There were a great number of transitional effects to shifting that we could not foresee. Until now, all that we were sure of was that all our shifts involving animals had not resulted in any neural trauma to the subjects. In fact, most animals showed superior neural functioning on several post-shift tests that we ran. More in depth conclusions on that must wait until later, but for the moment, we can conclude that the effect on neural systems is similar to that of a core dump of a computer. The difference is that in the case of Mike Colford the 'colour' and 'flavour' of his memories were transferred to Max as well. Essentially, his mind, not just the contents of his brain, was downloaded into Max."

"And while Max was programmed to ignore what might be considered irrelevant," Maureen resumed, "the download has set up a learning system. That is what accounts for the overly large core usage. Max has learned to be sentient."

"Hogwash!" Reall, retorted, his home town accent rising with his ire. "Y'all tryin' to tell me that your three trillion dollar computer now has a mind of its own. Impossible; why one of my committees has closed down four research projects, this year alone. All of 'em were tryin' to do just what you say happened here by accident."

"Actually, it is very possible, Senator," Mitch interjected, "The gel matrix of this model AI is based on nucleic acid transfer technology, very similar to that found in the brain's encoding system. As it acquires new information a nodal network forms in the core. This is also very much like at least one neurological model for human memory. And there is no other explanation for the rapid increase in the use of Max's core memory. And besides," Mitch added with an impish grin calculated to irk Reall, "Max told us."

The senator was just about to explode, once more, when General Urnbreach spoke up. His voice was quiet and his tone purposeful as he addressed Maureen.

"Does this mean that Max will no longer carry out instructions?"

Again Maureen was surprised by his deferential tone.

"While he won't respond like an unthinking automaton, I believe that Max will continue to work with us. In fact, I believe that he is highly motivated to do so. As I mentioned a moment ago, even as a simple AI, Max's 'personality' showed an affinity towards the Colonel. He did take the name 'Max' from the Colonel. Now, his dedication to Mike is total. He will do nothing that might endanger Mike or the project in any way. There are limits, however, to what he will relay to us about what is happening on the other resonance plane, if he feels that it's private in nature. He does relay all telemetry and technically relevant information."

"And who decides what's relevant?" Reall exploded.

"Max is quite capable," Mitch stated, very matter-of-fact, "after all, he contains every detail about this project, and the intelligence to use that information to everyone's best advantage."

"Great, now the computer is running the project."

"No he isn't!" Maureen stated with an emphasis that surprised even her. "Although he may have attained sentience, Max also learned loyalty. He will follow instructions. But at this point in the project, he is now best able to make certain judgments for which he didn't have the capacity before; judgments that might be beyond anyone else under certain circumstances. The probability of success of this mission has increased exponentially as a result of this 'accident'."

As the community roused itself from the evening's recreation, Aaron reappeared at Mike's side. He had disappeared, along with the others Mike had identified as probable leaders, right after the meal. Now he was back, as abruptly as he had left.

"Lights out," he informed Mike. "Come, we have prepared quarters for you here on the ground level," he said as he led Mike off to one side of the large outer cavern.

The room was sparsely decorated, just as one would expect, but it was obvious that some effort had been made to give it some little sense of warmth and comfort. Little by little, Mike was learning which things were important to a fugitive group forced into what was most likely would be permanent hiding.

"I should tell you," Aaron told him quietly, "that some of the 'Elders' have reservations about you. You can understand, I'm sure, that we cannot be too careful in our situation. They want to meet with you tomorrow. There are still many questions."

"I understand. I am curious about a great many things myself, but haven't had much chance to ask any questions at all."

"I know." the younger man answered with a shrug, to which Mike responded with an understanding smile. He could be patient. He was just a visitor here. For these people this was their way of life, their only way to survive.

"Just one other thing," Aaron added, "don't leave your room during the night unless you need the facilities, and if you do – straight there and back. At night the guards are especially watchful, and more than a little twitchy." He then wished

Mike a good night, and left him alone.

As soon as Aaron left the room Max 'spoke up', *"That was some evening. You did very well on the physics and chemistry of internal combustion and diesel engines. Remember, if you're ever stuck, you can always query my databases."*

"Right, Uncle Jim would really love that, he's probably already having fits of apoplexy worrying that I might accidentally divulge some of his precious secrets. Speaking of the General, what's he up to anyway, and how did you know to send that bus through to the parking lot?"

"The General, Mitch and Maureen have been in a meeting with Senator Reall from Washington for the last four hours."

"Sounds serious. What's up?"

"Well, I didn't want to tell you before; you were rather busy immediately following your arrival, but it seems that Mitch's worry about random harmonics wasn't as unfounded as the General thought. At the same time you shifted, so did a large part of the base, almost everything but the people, the nuclear containment facility, quartermaster stores, Hanger C, and the base's outlying houses. Your condo is safe, by the way."

"That explains the bus..," Mike cut in.

"Correct."

"But why did only one bus arrive here? Why not the whole motor pool?"

"The exterior harmonics were not planned, and were constantly shifting according to the harmonic variances that I created shifting you. I applied those harmonics all at once to shift you, but the dispersion field applied them randomly to the base's materiel. The most likely explanation is that the various parts of the base were scattered throughout various continua. There is no way to tell where each part went. You may yet turn up more pieces. And, as it happened, the Senator arrived just as the shift began. He was not pleased to find himself sitting naked on the ground at the front guard post. He was lucky that his limousine was stopped at the time it vanished."

"Did you say naked? "Mike couldn't help but chuckle at that fact. He'd never met the man, but he knew how much grief he had been giving his "uncle" the General. Max continued, "The harmonics were that pervasive?" I can see why the Senator would be upset. So now, they're trying to decide what to do about the missing base?"

"Yes and..," Max paused.

"And?" Mike asked.

"Me," Max told him, "Reall wants to pull my plug. Mitch purposefully left the conference room pick up turned on so I could listen in."

"It seems the Senator is worried about my loyalties, whether I will behave like a good 'computer' should, and follow my programs, or rather his programs, blindly. He wants Maureen and Mitch to transfer control of the project to the backup system at Twin Pines."

For a moment Mike was taken aback by the prospect. He was no expert, but, from his unique perspective, he was sure that Max, the friendly AI, had graduated from mere machine to something more resembling a living entity. You don't just shut off living beings.

"Thanks for the vote of confidence, for whatever its worth," Max replied to Mike's reflection. *"The team, General Urnbreach included, are impressing that fact on the Senator right now."*

"Don't worry," Mike responded resolutely, *"No one's going to turn off my spouse; certainly not while we're still on our honeymoon."*

"I'm still rather new at this," Max answered, *"but I think that was a joke, wasn't it?"*

"Maybe…" was all Mike said.

For a while afterward, Mike talked with Max, as his partner relayed to him the discussion underway in the control complex's conference room. When it seemed certain that they were not about to terminate what, almost everybody agreed, was a new life form, and when they had finally convinced the senator that Max was still the best AI to control the Shift Chamber, the discussion broke up. Everything that could be resolved on the spot had been. All that was left, was for the General to verify that the emergency provisions he had made to temporarily clothe and house the base personnel had been seen to, and to find transport to take the Senator back to his hotel suite in Burlington.

As Max wrapped up his report, Mike leaned back in the small chair stretching as much of his body as possible and yawned. It had been a long and difficult day, and it was fairly certain that nothing more was going to happen that night, and the bed, even if it was a little small, looked very inviting, Mike decided to call it a night.

The cool sheets felt good as Mike slipped between them. As he put his head on the pillow, he felt the lump of his 12mm automatic. His hosts were sincere enough in their welcome, but they were also a fugitive people. The General would not be too pleased if his first mission ended abruptly, with him being yanked home by Max wearing nothing but his boxers, because he allowed himself to be caught off guard.

Just as he was drifting off to sleep, he was suddenly wide awake again. He was instantly aware of Max's amplification of his senses as he heard the footfalls in the hallway. His hand closed on the butt of the pistol. The person in the hall paused. Mike lay still with his hand under the pillow. To a casual observer, he was asleep. Finally, almost silently, the person in the hall slipped into his room.

Jillian was barely dressed, and what she was wearing recalled vivid memories of the beauty that Mike already knew to be under her scant garment. It also reminded him of the woman he had left behind. Jillian approached without a word. The light footfalls of her bare feet on the stone floor accented the stillness in the room as she moved to sit on Mike's bed, even with his waist. She leaned forward pulling her feet up onto the bed, pressing herself close, in a move calculated to cause her garment to fall open.

"I owe you a great deal," she whispered. "You saved my father's life." Then she kissed him.

A wave of desire passed over Mike as her scent flooded his nostrils, instantly replaced by a sense of confusion. In that instant he answered Max's question of the night before. He really was in love with Gillian, the Gillian of his home world. Secondly, while Jillian was a virtual carbon copy of the woman he left standing in the control room door, when she kissed him he had no sense of the passion or desire that he had experienced that night with 'his' Gillian. It was all very new to him and something didn't fit.

Jillian sensed something was wrong, too. To Mike's surprise, she only paused for a heartbeat and then continued to make advances sliding her hands down inside the blankets. Then, when Mike still didn't respond he sat up again, pulling closed the little clothing she was wearing.

The look on her face was one of hurt, question and... *"Yes...,"* Mike thought, *"failure"*.

"You were sent, weren't you?" he asked, seizing her arms when she tried to rise.

"Yes," she responded softly. Jillian looked as though she was close to tears – genuine tears. Again Mike was puzzled. "Someone is waiting for your report?" he asked.

"Yes..."

He released her arms. "You were to find out if I was a spy or not?"

She nodded.

"Please," Mike asked softly, "wait for me outside while I dress." When Jillian didn't move right away he added, "There are questions. Your people need answers. They must be very important or else they would not have asked this of you. So, we're going to give them the answers that they need." He motioned toward the door. Without another word Jillian stood up and left the room.

As soon as she was gone, Mike got up and dressed very quickly. *"Listen close, Pal,"* he told Max, *"if this doesn't go well you may have to pull me back fast."*

"Always ready," came the reply. *"More and more like me all the time"* Mike thought. Max didn't reply.

Outside the room Jillian was waiting; so was the young man with the large blade he had met on his arrival. Mike accepted it with some measure of grace. A persecuted society, he reasoned, deserved a lot of latitude.

The young man indicated that Mike should precede him. He did. Jillian fell in beside Mike, silently. Whenever they came to a turning she took the lead. They didn't go very far, just around a corner and one level up, in a room above the one Mike had just left. As Jillian entered someone slipped a more substantial garment around her shoulders. The people that Mike had picked out as Elders were waiting around a table that seemed to have been hewn out of the rock itself, among them sat Aaron and Sam. They were only slightly surprised to see him. Mike surprised everyone by taking charge of their meeting.

"Friends," he began. He wasn't sure that it was the most reassuring opening, but it was the best he could come up with at short notice. "I can understand your fears. They must be great if you would ask such a thing of Jill." The young woman's look turned to one of surprise at his comment, but Mike didn't have time to elaborate. He had to move quickly if he was going to allay their fears.

Sam said, "We all do what we must – to survive." There was a resolve in his voice, but it was seasoned with a father's love and pride in his daughter's bravery as he glanced at her. Jillian remained silent.

"I understand," Mike continued, "but as much would have been gained if you had just asked me directly." A younger man across the table spoke up, "How could we have been sure that you would be telling the truth? This whole thing could be an elaborate Imperial plot to get information before you turn us all in to the Imperial Guard."

"Normally, one is never a hundred percent sure of any stranger, but it just happens that the differences between your world and mine are significant enough to be very convincing, Molly and Ruth and their colleagues would bear that out. I am sure that they have already given you a full report."

The various nods around the table confirmed his suspicions about the friendly grilling he had received from the scientific group. He could also see that the fact that he was not of their world had distressed them. So he began explaining his mission leaving out, of course, the technical details.

The meeting continued for quite a while, until the

council seemed satisfied with his explanation. Afterward, as Mike turned to leave Sam stood up, "We do believe you," he said, earnestly, "I apologize for trying to test you in that way. On behalf of the Council of Elders, be welcome, and again on my own behalf and that of my friends, thank you for our lives." He came forward as if he was going to shake his hand, but when Mike approached, Sam grabbed him and pulled him into an affectionate hug. Each member of the council did likewise in turn. They then bid him good night and he left with Jillian.

Jillian escorted him back to his room. There was, the elders admitted, one more matter that they needed to discuss. Mike was pleased to note, as they left the council room, that the guard was no longer waiting for them. Jillian noticed him looking around and reassured him.

"What father said was true. Although your story is very bizarre, there is evidence that actually supports it – particularly one other thing," she added enigmatically. "You'll see tomorrow – I'm sure of it." Mike asked what the "other thing" was. But Jillian told him that he would have to be patient. She repeated that she was sure that they would show him in the morning. Mike decided to leave it at that for the time being.

The pair walked in silence the short distance to his room. When they arrived she again surprised Mike by asking if she could come in for a minute. At first he wondered if this was going to be one last test, but the look on her face told him it wasn't. Although Jillian seemed somewhat nervous and uncertain there was no longer any hint of the 'seductress' about her. He stood aside and allowed her to enter.

Jillian crossed the small room and sat, nervously, on the end of the bed. She looked up at Mike with an almost plaintive expression. Mike sat down on the chair opposite her and waited for her to speak. For a long while she remained silent. He was just about to ask her what she wanted when Jill began, haltingly.

"When I first…uh…came to you earlier," she began, "umm, you seemed very eager, but only for a second, and then you went cold. I…uh…thought that …maybe you liked me. It looked that way when we first met this afternoon. I mean…well." then in despair, softly, "I'm not sure what I mean. Don't you like me?" The question was almost plaintive. It was obvious to Mike, now, that somehow they had connected and, in that instant, this Jillian had fallen in love with him. For a moment, he wondered if the Gillian back home had.

"Yes!" was all Max said, and then he was silent again.

Mike went over to Jillian and crouched down to her level. Taking both of her hands in his, he began to explain about the Gillian he'd left back in his own dimension, how he had fallen in love with her that first night and then spent the last month running away from the idea.

"Now I don't believe you." Jillian announced. "You're no coward. If you were, you would have gone back to your own world the moment you found yourself in the arena. But you didn't. You fought to save a group of people you didn't know, had never even seen before. You couldn't even be sure that it wasn't a legitimate execution. You could have been risking your life to get a bunch of criminals out of the city. How could you be afraid of love?"

Mike didn't bother to address the legitimacy of any execution, particularly one involving wild beasts and frenzied spectators.

"A very good friend of mine," he began, "a fellow physician, often calls me the last true 'Lothario'. You see, in my continuum in the latter half of our 20th Century an epidemic broke out. It was called AIDS – *Acquired Immune Deficiency Syndrome*. It was a disease that destroyed the body's immune system, totally. One of its primary methods of transmission was through sexual contact. For the longest time there was no cure. In the end, the real 'cure-before-the-cure' was education and understanding. People were forced to take a good look at how they perceived their sexuality and relationships. Everyone realized that it was time to grow up and stop playing with sex as if it was a toy, almost everyone, anyway.

"There have always been a few – like me – we just have to 'play the field'. Only when I met Gillian, something was different, very different. I just didn't want to admit it to myself, or to her. Partly, I was afraid to give up my illusion of emotional freedom, but I am slowly coming to realize that I was also afraid that she didn't feel the same. You see, back home I'm fairly well known; you might say I'm famous. I didn't know whether it was me she liked or my image, and I was afraid to find out. – Terrified, actually – she is very special. So I tried, very hard, to tell myself that she was just another "conquest". And you, you are so much like her. I mean you are her, but you're not, if that makes any sense..."

"I think so," Jillian said, though she wasn't totally sure. Jillian yawned. "I also think I'd better be getting to bed," she said, standing.

Mike rose with her still holding her hands. She pulled him to her and kissed him warmly, and then released him. As she was walking out the door she turned and said, "As soon as you get back you be sure and tell her, and if she doesn't want you any more, come right back here, because I do."

And then Mike was alone, again, his head was spinning. Not only had he come to an unbelievable realization tonight, he had actually said it out loud to another person.

"To a lot of other people, too, if I wasn't editing some of the 'goings on.'", Max informed him.

Mike jumped. He still wasn't used to the new Max. Then, the import of what Max had just said hit him. If this change hadn't occurred, Max would have followed the program and echoed every word and event onto a mission recorder.

"Thanks pal. What's between Gillian and I is between her and I, only. Not for some report that Senator Reall will be sending to Washington."

"Or general gossip about the complex by techies with little or no love life of their own," Max added, *"Besides, I am sure that you would prefer to tell Gillian yourself."*

"You're amazing, Partner." Mike told him, *"You have it all in a nutshell. Now, one last request, could you do whatever it was you did last night? I really need to get some sleep and my mind is spinning."*

"As requested," Max replied and Mike felt himself begin to fade. This time Max didn't reduce his audio input. Mike was not in a nice safe hospital room now. Max was not about to allow any danger creep up on him while he was asleep.

After the meeting with Reall finally broke up, and transport back to his hotel had been arranged for the Senator, General Urnbreach found himself walking past the control center just as Maureen Simms was leaving for the night.

"Dr. Simms," he said, in greeting, "I must admit that you stood up to the Senator rather well in there this evening. Jansen Reall and I have locked horns many times before this. He can be one ornery cuss."

"But can he cause us any real harm, General?"

"Oh yes! If he puts his mind to it, he can cause significant damage back in Washington. It is what I have been trying to avoid for a long time, why I have been pushing everyone so hard," he paused. "Come to think of it, I guess I've been pretty difficult to work with, haven't I, Dr. Simms?"

"It's Maureen," she corrected, "and you made up for it all tonight. At one point I thought that Reall was going to attack me physically. But you were right there." On impulse, she reached over and gave his arm an affectionate squeeze.

As they talked, the General walked with Maureen to the temporary quarters that he had arranged for her. A complement of soldiers on the base had done an excellent job getting up as many of the prefabs as they could manage since noon. Many of those same soldiers, Maureen knew, would be sleeping in tents that night. When they arrived at her door, she found that she didn't want the General to leave.

"It's chilly out tonight, General," she began, "would you like to come in for a minute? Sgt. Hennessey said that he was able to find me some powdered hot chocolate and a kettle."

The invitation caught the older man off-guard, and for a moment, he didn't know what to say.

"Maureen, I shouldn't. You know how rumors start. I mean I am old enough to be your father, at least."

Maureen put a hand to his mouth as if to stop him. "When I first met you," she told him, "I thought that you were the crustiest old fart anywhere. You could get me going so easily. So often, I was ready to kill. Then, as time went on, I started getting used to you. I found that I actually liked you. You are quite a man, quite a person. I promised myself that if you ever showed even one thread of humanity that I would grab onto you and hold on as long as you'd have me. Today, as we were preparing for the shift. I saw you, watching Mike. You were worried, concerned, for him."

"Colonel Colford and I have a long history," he told her, as if to pass it off as nothing. "Not only was his father one of my closest friends, I signed young Mike's enlistment papers after his dad was murdered. And, I'm his commanding officer. I am responsible."

"Bull. You might use that line successfully around the Pentagon, but I know otherwise. You were there for me tonight and I'm not really 'under your command'. You stuck up for all of us. And you even supported Max, and he's not even human."

"Yes, I suppose that I did, but..." Urnbreach began, hesitantly.

"No 'buts'. Sgt. Hennesey also told me that you were planning to bivouac with the men tonight. That's why, very quietly, I got Corporal Alders to find me an extra cot and I won't take 'no' for an answer."

"Maureen!" was the General's shocked reply, "What will people say?"

Maureen gave him her most mischievous smile, "Nothing, I'll just tell anyone who asks that my 'Dad' stayed over." And then she threw her arms around his neck and kissed him lightly on the cheek. When he made no move to resist she kissed him on the mouth. To her delight and his surprise, the General found himself returning the embrace, passionately.

When they finally broke, it was Maureen that looked about to see if they had been observed. She then slipped her hand in his and led him indoors.

"By the way, Maureen," he told her as he closed the door behind them, "off-duty, my friends call me 'James' or 'Jim.'"

Exactly six hours later, Mike awoke, refreshed and alert. Thanks, he knew, to the ministrations of Max, via his endocrine network.

"You're welcome," Max responded to his implied thanks.

"I think when I get back, I am going to throw my alarm clock out," Mike joked.

"That was a birthday gift from your fiend, Phil, he would never forgive you." came Max's retort, and he was right.

After dressing, Mike set off in search of three things: breakfast, Jillian, and the Council of Elders. As he turned into the large cavern everyone referred to as the "Main Hall" he found the last two. Actually, he found most everyone. The majority of the community was gathered there – apparently doing nothing. From the entry arch he looked for Jill and, finding her, he realized what everyone was 'doing'.

The wall of a small niche, off to one side, were coated with a luminescent algae that glowed in several shades of green and blue. But the glow that seemed to radiate from Jillian, by far, outshone it in beauty. Mike remembered another morning several weeks earlier, and regretted the time he had wasted running from the truth.

He scanned the room again. People of all ages: young children, adolescents, old people, all sitting there on chairs, cushions, mats or even the stone floor. They were all meditating, practicing what Gillian had called 'pure prayer'. The silence was profound. Mike couldn't help but be moved. When it was over the whole community rose quietly and, with a small bow of reverence seemingly to an empty niche at the front of the room, they all left. Only Mike didn't move. He stood, transfixed; until Jillian came up beside him.

"Good morning." she said, softly. "Have you been standing here long?"

"No. It seems that I have a knack for arriving just as people are finishing."

"Then, you are familiar with meditation?" Jillian asked. "Oh – yes – she meditates too, the other Gillian?"

Mike nodded, remembering that image, superimposing upon it the image of this morning's Jillian. "Seeing you reminded me of her, that's how I knew what you were all doing. It was amazing, the effect of seeing all of you there. Do you do that every morning?"

"Every morning and evening," Jillian responded "usually as a community, except when circumstances make it expedient for us to meditate in private."

"Like when you have to check out a strange new arrival."

Jillian blushed and Mike realized that she thought he was referring to the incident in his room the night before. To his surprise, Mike blushed, too. For some reason his discomfort made Jill feel better, she smiled, shyly.

"I really only meant that you needed to maintain the illusion of the 'welcoming home' party, so that Molly, Ruth and company could check me out. Though I find it comforting that you blush at the memory, it dispels any image of a wanton "Mata Hari" that may come to mind."

"A wanton what?"

"'Mata Hari', a somewhat larger than life spy on my world, during one of our last global wars. If you show me where breakfast can be found, I'll tell you all about her."

"Well, I'll show you where breakfast is, but your tales of espionage and intrigue will have to wait, I have to see my father before the Council of Elders meets again. And, just so you know, they will probably be sending for you again soon. You may find what they have to show you very interesting."

Just as Mike was about to ask what she meant by that they arrived back at the 'refectory'; where the community, that he had just observed in so profound a silence, was now buzzing about the very common business of getting breakfast.

"I'll see you again very soon," Jill told Mike, and with a quick peck on the cheek, she disappeared up a side corridor.

As before, her departure left Mike's head spinning. He got himself some breakfast and found an out-of-the-way table where he could eat and think at the same time. He fervently hoped that his new friends didn't think that he was snubbing them, but he still had so much to think about.

Although he was tempted to let himself dwell on his recent discoveries concerning his relationship with Gillian, what he had witnessed this morning stuck in his mind as a stark contrast to the savagery with which this people of peace was being treated. Jews in his world had, for centuries, been favorite targets of prejudice. But the utter barbarity of that arena spectacle, and the way that the populous accepted, perhaps even sought it, brought to mind the depravity of the Holocaust. How could this be? And more, what, if anything, could he do about it?

"I will need more data to be able to help you with that question," Max interjected.

Until then, Mike had not realized that Max hadn't spoken to him since he'd woken up. *"Good morning, Partner. Where have you been?"*

"Right here, as always. I didn't think you needed me, and you do need some space of your own – so I gave it to you. Also, I was busy with Mitch and the physics team. They are fascinated by the information that we provided them with, concerning the transport system. Mitch believes that they probably never developed the idea of the wheel as a mode of transport, beyond the horse and cart, if that, but somehow, very early on, they happened on elementary electro physics. From the stage of development you observed, it appears that they left their horses and carts behind quite a long time ago. General Urnbreach wants you to get as much technical information as you can. He says that whatever you can get, he can use to control the damage Senator Reall might try to inflict. Reall's really giving everyone a hard time. The General is worried. He won't say so, but it shows. Strangely enough, the one person who seems most concerned about him is Maureen. She is always exchanging glances with him, when they think that no one is looking. Weren't they always at odds before?"

"Stranger things have happened," Mike responded, *"Like computers learning to assess moods and make value judgments, for instance."*

"Good point," Max replied. *"So what's next?"*

Before Mike could answer, Jill returned.

"Still eating?" she asked, looking down at Mike's plate.

Following her gaze, Mike realized that he had barely touched his food. "Lost in thought", was all he said at first. Later, after he wolfed down his breakfast, Jill gave him a tour of the caves.

"The original escapees found these caves when they first managed to elude their handlers on one of the scrub-clearing assignments, about two hundred years ago," she explained. "Ever since, select members of our community, people like Aaron, have been making forays back into the city for supplies and to free other slaves. Sometimes, like Aaron, they get caught and thrown in the arena. He was caught while trying to free Molly, that's how he ended up there.

"When the first escapees found the cave, the main chamber was a natural formation, although the cavern you see today has been enlarged quite a bit. So too, were many of the other original chambers. They only had pick axes and sledge hammers that they were able to liberate from other work sites in the city on those night-time raids. The walls were polished using the pieces of stone that they chipped away…"

"Much like the way one uses a diamond to polish another diamond," Mike observed.

"I'm afraid that I know little of that process, although, as you can see, it did work very well here." Jillian ran her hand over the smooth stone. Mike saw that the stone face actually had a kind of sheen.

As they moved from one location to the next, Mike explained that he couldn't understand how the authorities could get away with such savagery as in the arena.

"There have always been such games, for over a thousand years." Jillian informed him. "A long time ago, the old Roman Government found it could serve two purposes. The arena 'games' kept the masses entertained, and satisfied their aggressive needs on the one hand, and very efficiently eliminated "undesirable elements" on the other. Even though the weight of its corruption eventually crushed the original empire giving way to the pseudo-democracies of the first century CE, that preceded the current New Roman Empire, the arena remains. It still serves whoever rules, with ruthless efficiency."

"CE?"

"Common Era – It was declared by the "New Romans" about sixty years after the death of the Emperor, Julius Caesar. It was meant to signify the beginning of the "New World Order" under Rome. That order lasted only another seventy-five years, but the calendar stuck, as did the name 'New Roman'. The name was useful to ensure the illusion of continuity and allow the patricians to continue asserting their superiority. The calendar was kept because it proved reliable for many other things, and it has been in use ever since. The Christians use a calendar based on the same system, which begins at the same time, but they refer to it as A.D., *anno domini*, referring to the time of Jesus of Nazareth, who they claim to be the Son of God."

"And what year is it now?" Mike asked.

"It's 961 CE, or AD, if you wish," Jillian responded as she turned the corner ahead of Mike, turning into a room marked "Infirmary".

"The surprises keep on coming," Mike thought to himself, not quite sure how to reconcile the level of technology he had seen in the city with the fact that this was supposed to be only the mid-tenth century. Then he followed Jillian into the infirmary and all doubt vanished.

Although the place was as spotless as any hospital ward he had ever seen, the similarity ended there. There were no IV's. He saw no traction or evidence of the technology to which he was accustomed. Most shocking, was the level of pain evident on the faces of the patients, as if they had no access to analgesics and sedatives. Then a scream came from an adjacent room. Instinctively Mike responded. What he found were three large men holding a fourth man down as a surgeon began to amputate his leg without any apparent anesthetic.

The obvious state of their medical knowledge was at par with a period before the tenth century of his world. Mike could see that gangrene in the leg was well advanced, and wished that there was a way to save the leg, but without 21st century pharmaceuticals there was nothing he could do. One thing he could do, though, was to help ease the patient's pain. Without saying a word, he reached into his emergency pack and withdrew his neuro-stimulator. Placing the electrode patches just behind the man's ears, he introduced a micro-current into his Raphe nucleus. Instantly, the patient was asleep.

The surgeon's first reaction was shock, until he saw the regular rhythm of his patient's breathing. He didn't know what Mike had done, but Mike could see that he was glad that he had done it, as he hurried to finish his task, afraid that this miracle sleep would wear off as suddenly as it had occurred. When the operation was complete, Mike reset the neuro-stimulator to release a long-acting endorphin into the man's system (At least he hoped that was what he'd done. He couldn't be positive that human neurology here was the same as in his own world.) He informed the surgeon, and promised to return later with complete explanation as Jillian hurried him away for another meeting with the Council of Elders.

Jillian rushed Mike out of the surgery and out of the infirmary through a tunnel that was leading them deeper into the cave network. Shortly, they came upon the council members, waiting for them at the end of the corridor. Aaron spoke first. "You were wondering why it is that we accept your story despite its rather fantastic nature," he began, "well, part of the answer is in this room, and there is even more outside." He stood away from the only door off that section of hallway and motioned for Mike to enter. When he did as requested, Mike found himself in a room full of plascrates, some of which had been opened.

"They just arrived, about the same time that we were told you arrived in the arena," one of the other elders explained. "What we had to be sure of was that they were not some sort of elaborate government trap to trick us into showing our presence. As you can surmise, that would be another explanation of the coincidence of your arrival."

Mike nodded, seemingly lost in thought which was actually conversation.

"No need to guess where from," Max put in. Mike mentally nodded his agreement, adding, *"Or at what time."*

The crates were all marked US AIR FORCE. Mike was sure that he was looking at a substantial portion of the base armory's stock.

"The serial numbers on the crates check out," Max informed him.

"I don't know if there is any way that we can send them back," Mike responded, *"but I do know that with them, these people would have a decent chance of defending themselves."*

"I don't know if they will get the chance, Mike. I had to tell the General right away, obviously, and he is already talking about ordering you back while you are in the same room just on the chance that they might return, too."

"And what if he does and they don't return? Then there is no one here to teach them how to use them, and if this hideout is found, then the government, here, gets a whole new arsenal, and it has the resources to figure them out for themselves."

"The General says 'Argument accepted. Give it a shot. We'll try and make sure that Reall doesn't find out.' And then he added to Maureen, in what he thought was a low enough voice, 'The PTB's at the Pentagon have been trying to get him into combat for years, and now he is doing it for himself.'"

Mike groaned, inwardly. '*Well, if I must...,*' he resolved.

The next couple of hours were spent cataloging and explaining each of the weapons. In one corner, there were a few plascrates that he found made him sorry that he didn't have one of the new 'Hellbat' attack helicopters available. Those crates, he told Aaron, were the newest most advanced smart missiles; designed especially for the Hellbat.

"Would that be a bulbous craft with three horizontal blades on top, a tube projecting out the back with a vertical set of blades, and the word '*Hellbat*' emblazoned on each side, in a burst of fire?"

Mike couldn't believe the luck – having both the craft and its weapons arrive in the same continuum, the odds were beyond imagination.

"*The General says that they are a little frightening, too,*" Max told him.

"We can use these, too?" Aaron asked, expectantly, when he read the expression on Mike's face in response to his description of the helicopter.

"I can," Mike told him. "I don't know if we would have the time to train someone else to fly the Hellbat. Can I see the bird?"

"Certainly," Sam answered. "But, first there is something else that we need to show you."

He motioned for Mike to precede him once more. Behind him Mike heard one of Sam's companions say to another, quizzically, "Bird?"

Already experiencing an emotional overload, Mike didn't even want to try and guess what was coming next as he was led down a corridor and out another of the cave network's hidden entrances.

Aaron and Sam led him across a small field toward a grassy knoll. As they came closer to the small hill Mike could see that it was actually a really great camouflage job. Sure enough, when they arrived Aaron pushed aside a mass of vines to reveal a door. This time, Mike was not even surprised when he noticed that the wall surrounding the door was plascrete and the window was made of translux steel. It was obviously a back door, Mike noticed, as there was only the number on the door, not the name of the facility, though that number seemed very familiar. As soon as he stepped inside the reason for that familiarity was clear. Down the left corridor, second turn to the right led to his office. He was in the camp's medical facility. If finding the weapons had made Mike happy, finding the Medical Centre here brought him close to delirium.

"This changes everything," Mike told the Elders after he gave them a tour of the facility. The weapons are one thing, but they are a finite resource. I doubt that there are any facilities readily available to you where you could make more. Once those are gone, that's it. The real value is in this building; our base hospital. Even the ruling class will fall in behind you, if you can promise them medical care that is centuries ahead of anything they now have. Imagine doing heart transplants or knee replacements. It is all within your grasp.

"In the hospital is a comprehensive medical library as well as something we call "CATS" that's 'C.A.T.S.'. That stands for 'Computer Aided Training System'. It's a system that can be programmed to teach a wide variety of subjects. The system here in the hospital is programmed to teach Medicine. Your physicians already have a basic understanding of rudimentary medical practice. If I teach them how to use CATS, they will have the knowledge to advance medical practice by more than a thousand years, practically overnight. Your world, undoubtedly, has the technology to reproduce the necessary medical equipment using the diagrams and instructions contained in the CATS programming. If you can provide the people with a level of medical care that is centuries ahead of what they have now, they would force their own government to grant you freedom. They might even overthrow the current government, if it resists.

"Don't be so sure," Gabriel told him "There are many slaves pressed into service because of their talents. Very often, slaves are educated to serve in particular capacities. Molly, who you met when you first arrived, was educated to be a university professor because they had no one among the Patricians willing to pursue the rigorous study of her discipline. All of the technically advanced people here, including our medical personnel, are escaped or rescued slaves.

"Society is used to having slaves to do whatever they need done. The Patricians, particularly, would stand behind the status quo and against the freeing of slaves or giving status to any non-Patricians. You may have noticed that they did not hesitate to throw Molly in the arena when it suited their purpose."

"So then we have no choice," Mike concluded, "the current system must fall. If I understand what I have been told of your political history correctly, it would appear that your world very similar to mine during our time of empires. That most likely means that all power rests with the Emperor." Two or three councillors nodded. "So if he surrenders, whomever he surrenders to, will become the new Emperor. We have the weapons to force his surrender right here and, from what I have seen, the government has little or no defense against them."

"We still have two major problems to resolve," Sam said. "The first is the other faiths. You see, Mike, we Jews are not alone. All religions, other than the state 'religion', are banned. Christians, Hindu, Buddhist and even those who do not wish to practice a faith, the non-theists, we are all treated the same. You encountered us because you 'landed' in this region.

"Each group of believers is interned in a different geographic location. We Jews were shipped here to the western continent because our homeland, in the middle eastern lands, is sacred to us, the land promised to our father Abraham. Our homeland is now populated by those who follow the Buddha. The northern portion of this continent, as well as Britannica and Gaul and some parts of what we call 'Europe' are now 'home' to the Christians.

"We don't have the manpower to move against the government, even with these new weapons; even if you train us to use them. The other groups will have to agree, to whatever your plan may be, before we can move forward. The Hindu and Buddhists tend to be very pacific, and while the Christians are fairly united, there is at least one faction that may resist following anybody but their own leaders. That group is also very militant, if they learn of the weapons cache, before they are on-board, they may try to subdue us, and take the weapons."

Mike thought about what he said, "Where is the Imperial Seat?"

"About 665 miles south west of here," Aaron answered.

"And is the governing body, whatever it's called, presently sitting?"

"The next 'Imperial Session' of the Senate begins at the end of the summer, in just over two months."

"Will the Emperor be present?"

"Of course, he'll be there to keep an eye on the Senate and the Regional Governors." Aaron told him. "He would be foolish not to. You can never be sure when the senators might decide to plan a coup. It happened with Caesar. You can bet he will be there and with a heavy security presence."

"Well, then that is when we seize power. Though, like I said already, that is just the beginning. The real ticket to freedom is still this Med Center. 'Modern Medicine', the promise of increased longevity and quality of life – the information in the CATS training system – that is the key to winning over the people and they are the key to keeping your freedom. If you are the official government, and you have the means to offer the populous a better life, if and only if they back you, then you have more than a chance. Do the other faiths you mentioned have resistance groups like this one, and can you contact them?"

"We do have a communication system with the other resistance groups," Sam affirmed. "We have already sent them word to send their representatives for a summit to discuss some new developments. They should begin arriving shortly."

"Then that leaves only the more important question for us to answer..." the speaker was an old man at the back of the room, who had listened intently to the on-going discussion. His name was Ezra.

When he spoke up, everyone in the room fell silent, almost as if it had been the voice of God, himself, that had spoken.

After a respectful moment, Mike quietly asked, "And that question is?"

No one spoke. All eyes focused on Ezra, reverently silent, already knowing what he was going to say.

Mike waited, too.

Ezra spoke directly to Mike. When he did, Mike felt the old man's voice flow into him, like a stream flowing out of a clear, calm lake.

"In the beginning of our history, we were slaves. But we were delivered from that, by the Almighty, his name be praised forever more. (*'So far just like back home.'* Mike thought.) Only, as soon as we were freed from the yoke of our oppressors, a large number of our people rebelled against the word of the Lord of our deliverance and his prophet Moses. Their act of rebellion brought disaster upon the community of fugitives.

"We were primitive, in those days, and we believed this catastrophe was a divine punishment. As we have grown, as a people, we have learned that he is a forgiving God. It is when we try to do things that we know are not in keeping with his way, when we are pursuing our own egos, this is the source of our disaster. Over and over throughout our history, when we put our trust in him things worked. When we harden ourselves against what we know to be moral, ethical and honest, in short, when we follow the 'quick-fix' impulse of the ego, we experience disaster.

"The extreme violence you propose seems very much like a quick-fix. To kill, particularly with these weapons that our adversary can't possibly expect and has no defense against – it's like slaughtering sheep. Can we justify it?"

Mike was taken aback by the holy man. His first impulse was to jump up and deny the argument as pious clap trap, but his experiences with Ezra's people wouldn't let him. He had seen how much their faith meant to them – not their religion as a collection of dogmas and doctrines, but their internal, intuitive faith in a real God. He wasn't sure how to answer. *"Any ideas, Max?"*

"Still not enough data, Mike. Try to get some printed data, history books, political science and technology texts or scientific papers, as many as you can."

"But I haven't enough time to read a whole lot of

material."

"You don't have to. I can use your eyes as a scanner and digest the books as fast as you can turn the pages."

Mike hadn't thought of that. He turned to Aaron, who was sitting next to him, as a small buzz rose in the room in response to Ezra's words.

Aaron told him that they had a makeshift library of books smuggled out of libraries and schools in the city. He then expressed the same comment that Mike had made to Max about the time that any serious reading would require.

"It's OK," Mike told him, "I'm a speed reader." Not entirely true, but it saved him trying to explain his neural implants. They would eventually know anyway, when they access the complete medical data bank at the Med Center, but he would be long gone by then and wouldn't have to spend a lot of valuable time answering the inevitable barrage of questions.

As the discussion in the room became more structured, concretely examining the moral and ethical question that Ezra had asked, Mike suggested that he would be better able to address that concern if he were better informed, and asked to be shown to their repository of books to begin his research.

Before leaving, he stopped beside Ezra. "I don't know enough about your world and your culture. I need to learn more. Can we talk again after I have done some research?"

The old rabbi agreed, and Mike followed Aaron to the

library.

Mike's research went very quickly, thanks to Max. Even so, it still took several days. As they moved from book to book Max kept Mike informed of each new discovery.

"It appears that this civilization has benefitted from the mathematics and engineering of the early Egyptian and Greek cultures that were lost in our world. That knowledge was considerable. The advanced math and engineering of the early cultures allowed for the very early discovery of basic electrical and electro-physical principles. These, in turn, led to the eventual discovery of superconductor technology about twelve hundred years ago. The hover vehicles, we saw in the city, are the oldest form — a thousand years old or so — of the three basic types of conveyance. The other two are magnetically propelled trains, similar to our mag-lev technology, and a trans-oceanic vessel that is a cross between a hover craft and a hydrofoil. The text is not specific as to how this is achieved. In fact, I am extrapolating from a very vague description. What is notable, however, is the lack of any real growth in these areas in several centuries."

"In terms of weaponry, all are of the energy-pulse type that we witnessed in the city. Variations of the same idea are used as tools of excavation and demolition. What Ezra said is true. They would have little or no defense against high explosives or the state-of-the-art assault weapons from our continuum. If we went ahead with an all-out assault we could slaughter them, with unconscionable collateral damage. It would be Central Park many times over."

"What about the force fields we saw at the arena?"

"Limited, not like your technology at all. They will hold back an individual or a group, because the field reacts at the point of contact with a matching force. However, bullets and missiles, even their slow moving air cars, move faster than the field's response can handle. They wouldn't be any defense against a hand grenade or mortar. Not only that, but most of the medium to large city defensive systems are centrally powered. Take out or overload the main power sources and you're home free. The same goes for communications, as well. Although, I am sure that the global capital will be much better protected vis-à-vis this world's technologies, it is just as vulnerable to our weaponry."

"Still, that does suggest some possibilities, anything else useful?" Mike mused.

"Well, you were right about the power structure. Change of government or failure to do so is decided by the strength of a given challenger. Over time, successive governments have taken greater and greater precautions to prevent hostile takeovers, including the decision that moved the Imperial capital here, to what is analogous to our North America. One certain key is their communications system. Nothing goes out over the air unless it is cleared by the imperial government. They have microwave communication – voice and data – all access to which is by government issued pass-code." Max told him.

"That could be a bit sticky. Still, it also increases our chances of success. I've got an idea forming. I want you to pass it along to the General and get his opinion."

The General didn't like Mike's idea very much at all. Not because it was a bad plan, but because it would make this, originally simple, reconnaissance mission a great deal more dangerous than anybody had foreseen or planned on. It would also stretch it out for more than eight weeks. Also, the plan called for Mike to take the Hellbat, in stealth mode, right down to the capital, in advance of the mission.

"Everything is controlled from the Ministry of Information. All the servers are there." Mike explained via Max. "The chances are that they have never even heard of a hacker. Your three-year-old grandnephew could probably crack their system. With Max's help, it should be a piece of cake."

"What do you hope to get from their servers that is so important?" The General asked.

"Everything involving security for the upcoming session of the Imperial Senate: Security codes; passwords for communications; the format of the passes and ID's used by the security forces; also uniform and insignia design for the Imperial Security personnel, and anything else that we will need to infiltrate the session. If all goes well we should have the Emperor's surrender before the end of the first day."

"That's if you can get the Helbat in and out of the capital without getting caught." The General observed.

"I think that I have a serious edge arriving soon. They tell me that a member of one of the Christian groups is coming here may have information that would give me the inside scoop on the whole setup. I'll know more once I've talked to him. In the meantime, anything that you can think of that would help us to get in and out without having to hurt anyone would be very valuable," Mike told the General.

"I'll see what I can do. Do you have any information on the setup, or the layout of the city?"

Mike smiled to himself, "Max has it all," he said. "It's not much yet, but if you can get any ideas from what is there, that would certainly be a help."

After he finished conferring with the General, Mike returned to his work. Though, as he reviewed the information that Max had gleaned from the library Mike was constantly running into walls. Many times he found no analogs to the government or command structures he was used to having in place.

"This is only 950 CE," Mike reminded himself with each anomaly. It was like he had travelled back in time, yet even that was not the whole problem. The extreme differences between this world and his were really making planning tricky. Still, Mike was confident that the direction his planning was going in would work. He really wanted to keep his promise to the elderly rabbi.

As he worked on his plans, Mike remembered Ezra's visit to him that second evening. While everyone else shared some community time after the evening meal, Mike had returned to the library to continue his research. As he was taking another book from the shelf the old rabbi joined him. He was so quiet that Mike didn't realize that he was standing there until he turned around.

"Good evening, Michael" Ezra began, his voice exuding peace and tranquility; Mike was swept up in it again.

"Rabbi, good evening," he replied. "Is there something that I can do for you, or were you just looking for a book? If that's so, please don't let me get in your way," he added with deference.

"You are most kind, Michael, but I came to talk with you. Is this a good time? I can come back if you wish."

"You can't help but love him, can you?" Max said. Mike was learning to accept value judgements from his AI friend. He agreed with him, too. Ezra had a way of touching people.

"Now is just fine, Rabbi," Mike told him. "How might I be of assistance?"

"I need to be sure that you understand my position on this use of violence," Ezra answered. Mike nodded, and the Rabbi continued. "One of the things that your faith and ours holds in common is the love of peace, also the belief that we are responsible for the good of our fellow human beings." Again Mike nodded.

"For over nine hundred years, the New Roman Empire has ruled: even longer than that, we have been slaves to Rome – since before the time of your prophet Jesus. We have struggled not only to survive as a race, but to remain faithful to our God." He paused for a moment, collecting his thoughts.

"In the book of the Psalms, King David repeats over and over that our help comes from the Lord. He is our salvation and our strength. He is why we have lasted for more than a millennium under Roman rule; even though our Imperial masters are getting more and more oppressive with each new Emperor. This is the point.

"In spite of everything that we have suffered and continue to suffer, we endure, in some ways we are even thriving. This is because we have been true to our faith and our traditions. We thrive because we live in the house of the Lord, no matter where in the world we might be." He pointed to his heart. "The real Temple is in here. Our God is with us because his name is written on our hearts.

"I know that a coup cannot be achieved without some violence. Even King David had to fight to keep his throne. The problem is how one uses force to secure victory. In David's day, everyone had the same weapons. That is no longer true. You say that you may be able to find a way to protect our people against their weapons, but what do the New Romans have to protect themselves against yours? If you attack in your Hellbat 'bird-thing', then it is possible that many innocent people may be injured or killed. Can we really do this and still be true to our God?

"There is a question that was asked by your prophet: 'What profit a man if he gains the whole world and loses his soul?' That is what I am afraid of happening to our people. Can we do this and still sit in prayer when it is done? Will we still be able to face our God when the battle is over?"

Anyone else, Mike had thought, and he would have dismissed him as living in a fantasy world. This was not the case with Ezra. Mike could feel his sincerity, the depth of his belief. That was when Mike had promised the venerable rabbi that he would do everything he could to ensure that the holy man's fears would not be realized.

Key to his plan was taking the Emperor, of course. If they could do it on the opening day of the Senate, the Regional Governors would be in the Senate Chamber that day as well. He could force a global surrender in a single strike and avoid a bloody conflict entirely. There would be some resistance. It was now his job to be sure that it was kept to a minimum.

If they could rally the manpower, and if their training went well, they could be ready to move within the eight week time frame. After all, as Ezra had said, this world's military had no defense against automatic weapons, gas grenades, or even simple handguns. Mike found himself fervently hoping that he could keep the promise that he had made to the old man of God. A possibly impossible task, but one that Mike Colford fervently believed in. Despite the General's comment, he was still a healer, not a destroyer. He was hoping to heal a world.

"He's really not comfortable with it you know, Jim," Maureen once reminded the General, as they walked along the lake bordering the camp one evening. "...even though it's his plan."

"I know. He has spent his entire Air Force career avoiding violence or working hard to stem its ravages – you should have seen him during the aftermath of the Park riots of '70. He hated to lose a single patient despite the fact that so many were 'more dead than alive' when they brought them into his makeshift M.A.S.H. The gangs had gotten their hands on some AK-62's, and what those do to the human body you don't want to see. He was the chief surgeon at the M.A.S.H.

we set up at the south end of Central Park. You know, one week he worked for six days straight – other than short naps, he didn't stop till that offensive was over. No, I don't imagine that he likes any of this – at all," Urnbreach concluded, and then fell silent.

"And you don't like seeing him in this position, either, do you?" Maureen thought to herself.

"Do you think," he asked after a time, "that we might be able to send him some kind of specialized help?"

"Not more people, if that's what you mean. We're not sure how Max would handle more neural interfaces. After what happened when Mike shifted, we could cause him to develop the AI equivalent of multiple personalities, or worse. He could shut down entirely," Maureen said.

"No, not people, but I just remembered something that he could use. I guarantee it would reduce casualties. C'mon," he said, suddenly very excited. "Let's go talk to Mitch." And then, without waiting for Maureen to reply, the General turned around and headed back to the control complex, seemingly oblivious to the fact that he was still holding Maureen's hand, or that she had to run to keep up with him.

That the General was still holding Dr. Simms hand when the pair dashed into the control room, raised more than a few eyebrows. Oh, there had been rumors bandied about of late, but no one believed them, nor dared test them. It was the General's high level of energy and excitement that really shocked them. It was, to say the least, most uncharacteristic of him. That he was still holding Maureen's hand and was addressing her by her first name, too, but neither behavior seemed to bother him, in the least.

"Craig," he bellowed from the door, "I was telling Maureen, here," he continued, when Mitch joined them from his office, "about the Colonel during the '70 riots, when I got an idea – something that might help him over there. "

All at once, Urnbreach dropped his voice to a near whisper, and directed the two of them towards his own office. He closed the door, and ignoring the stares that he was getting through the full-length windows that looked out onto the control room, he launched into his idea.

"We never told anyone about this, for obvious reasons," he began in a mock conspiratorial tone, "but they used a new kind of stun gas in Central Park in 2070. If the Pentagon hadn't stumbled on this stuff by accident a few months earlier, the losses there could have been much greater. Why they didn't deploy it sooner I'll never know. It might have been because the project that developed it wasn't originally sanctioned by the brass – it was just a couple of guys in 'Covert Weapons' doing some anti-terrorist research, when they had a very interesting accident.

"It was with a gas, a variant of *Axon-D*..."

"What!" Mitch nearly hit the ceiling. "To reduce casualties?! That stuff is the deadliest stuff the Pentagon ever developed..." In his excitement, Mitch raised his voice causing many of those just outside the office door to turn and look through the glass. Hurriedly, the General hushed him up.

"Quiet – and let me finish. I said that this was something new, didn't I? These two think-tankers had been working on a project that they set for themselves – to play with over lunch. It was just an intellectual exercise at first, trying to find a way to detect the presence of the gas, while it was still in the canister – something about how its muons would interact with the mesons of the container."

"That would make sense," Mitch said, "*Axon-D* destroys nerve axon transmission by causing a complete depolarization along the membrane. Although, even the creators aren't sure how it works, it is suspected that it inhibits electron transfer in both sodium and potassium atoms. It stands to reason that the compound could also be fairly active at the sub atomic particle level."

The General gave Mitch a long stare, so did Maureen. It was as if this was a stranger among them, not a known co-worker.

"We scientists have our network," he said, matter-of-factly, in response to the unasked question. "Obviously, we just don't talk about it."

"Obviously," the General replied with a touch of sarcasm. "Anyhow, while trying to find a way of keeping this stuff from ending up on planes or space shuttles and the like, they tried polarizing the gas canisters with magnetic fields of different frequencies. At one point, just after they had adjusted the field to a new setting and activated it, the lights went out, for everyone, throughout most of the building. They were out for at least three hours. When they came around, the two geniuses analyzed the residue in the test chamber and found that, at the frequency that they used, the molecule of *Axon-D* wasn't polarized. Rather, it was converted to a form of radio energy that was propagated to a radius proportional to the volume of gas used. Once it reached maximum range, it re-converted to matter once more. Only then, was the molecule polarized to the frequency that they had intended, and in its polarized condition, it only knocked everyone out, no one was harmed otherwise. Not only that, but further research found that the standard inoculant against the original gas works for this variant. The only catch is that, in the presence of a strong enough magnetic field of any other frequency, the *Axon-D* re-materializes, instantly, in its original, highly lethal form."

"And you want to send Mike some of this modified gas and the inoculant?" Mitch asked.

"Don't you think that it will work, or is there a problem in shifting it?"

"No, not in shifting it… it's just those damned aircars. They are bound to be putting out one fierce magnetic field."

"Oh, right," the General replied, instantly deflated.

"Cheer up, Jim," Maureen whispered in his ear, "It was an inspired idea. It's just that physics got in the way."

"And you did solve the 'Mystery of Government Lab P'," Mitch added. "For me, at least," he quickly added, as the General gave him a warning look.

"Craig," he said, "you're going to be the death of me

yet," but the momentary repartee had partially restored his mood.

If Mike had known that the next day would have turned out the way it did, he would have stayed in bed, or at least that's what he told himself that night as he wearily headed for his bed. On the third day, after he began his research, the first of the other resistance groups had arrived: The very reactionary and militant Christian sect he had been told about. They were a smaller splinter group that was made up, mostly, of the descendants of the Jewish Zealots of the first century BCE, who had converted to their own idea of Christianity. This small group still believed, like their ancestors, that they had to win their freedom by force, and that "Divine Providence" meant that God would help them slay their foes so that "...His will be done!...."

They had been responsible for more retaliatory and punitive actions, taken by their rulers against the captive populations than, any other group. Mike learned that most of the group that he had rescued from the arena on the day he arrived had been condemned in retaliation for one of the Zealot attacks on a Roman patrol. Had they been told of them on their arrival, the Christian zealots would have been all for taking the new weapons and levelling the capital.

When the council chose to begin by introducing them to the new medical technology, they refused to accept it. They rejected the idea of using this new technology to secure their place with the New Romans. They believed the concept of surgical intervention was a ploy of the government, to trick them into defiling the body, the "Temple of the Holy Spirit".

Apart from necessary amputations, which they held to be brought about as a divine punishment, and therefore God's work, they believed that the human body should not be cut. Somehow or other, though, they still believed that tearing the hell out of it with a jagged blade would be perfectly acceptable – so long as it was a heathen body.

This also meant that they were very suspicious of Mike. They "called" him before their group and grilled him extensively, despite protests by Aaron, Sam and the others. By the time they were through, he had felt very "wrung out" and wanted to get as far out of their way as possible. He still hadn't finalized his plan to take the capital without any serious number of casualties – a plan that the Zealots would surely not agree with. "Death to the heathen!" was their raison d'être. To get them to see things Ezra's way (and his), Mike concluded, was definitely going to require some "divine providence".

He went back to the library, and emptied a shelf of books onto the table, returning to his role as the human document scanner, turning page after page each time Max requested *"Next"*.

"I have noticed something interesting..," Max began, just as Mike picked up the sound of movement outside the door. Max, of course, heard it too, and paused. Mike's hearing was, at once, enhanced. But the sounds of movement had stopped. Then Mike heard the sound of bare feet on stone, and he remembered his first night. The Zealots really didn't trust him, and, as it turned out, they were as subtle as a sledgehammer. For within a few seconds, Anna, a young, very attractive member of their group appeared in the doorway. From her

appearance, she was barely out of childhood, no more than eighteen or nineteen. Mike could see, by the determined way she moved, that she was there on a mission. More so than it was with Jillian, this serving girl, Anna, was ill-equipped to handle her assignment. She had no idea what she was supposed to do.

When she entered the room, Anna was wearing a long cloak covering her body to her ankles. Two steps inside the door, and she unfastened the clasp at her throat, letting the cloak fall to the floor revealing her naked form. Naked she was, too. The person before him was, in all ways that mattered, a little girl, an innocent ordered to be a seductress, whose only plan was to appear, let him see her bare body and expect to be ravaged by the person who her people believed to be an imperial spy.

"Maybe that's why they used her," Max suggested. *"If you really were a hedonistic imperial spy, that is what you would do, isn't it? She lets you see her body and you do the rest – Q.E.D. They prove their case, at least as far as they are concerned. I guess, in their minds, if you are virtuous, you only abuse young women by sending them to be molested."* To Mike, Max was sounding both indignant and sarcastic, and he agreed with every word.

Although with Jillian Mike had been as gentle as he could, he had already had his fill of these "ham-handed" rebels. This blatant misuse of a young girl, who was such an innocent, infuriated him.

Mike's first impulse was to take his anger out on the girl. He was just mad enough to let it get the better of him, too. Yet, there she was so vulnerable and frightened. Anna stood before him, trembling. She wasn't nude, she was horribly naked. Mike stayed his anger, and as gently as he could, he said. "Forget it, kid," and returned to the book that he and Max were working on. He hoped that his matter-of-fact rebuff would be enough.

It didn't work. Anna had her orders. She was to prove that this person was really a government spy sent to deliver all of them into the Imperium's power. "Why else," it had been reasoned, "would he advocate desecration of the body and call it healing – only God heals." That, for the zealots, had been reason enough, the girl had been sent.

So in spite of Mike's dismissal, Anna didn't leave. Although intent on his task, Mike was very aware of her, standing close by. He tried to appear as though he was totally oblivious to her presence, as he continued to scan the text. Anna waited a few moments, then, hesitantly, she crossed the room to where he was working.

Anna brushed up against his back, pressing close, slipping her arms around his chest. "You read very fast," she whispered in his ear, "I hope that's the only thing that you do that fast." The words were meant to be seductive, but to Mike's ear they sounded mechanical. She began to nibble his earlobe. Mike put down the book and turned to face her, eye to eye. He saw fear and determination. She had been pressed into service, and was determined to succeed at any cost. Mike felt his anger growing again. *'How do they reconcile this abuse with their fundamentalist beliefs?'* he asked himself. He tried to pry her arms away from his body, but she clung to him, pressing her lips to his in an attempt to kiss him. That was when Jillian had decided to drop by to see how his research was coming along, and to bring him a light snack. From the door, it seemed to her that Mike and the girl were engaged in a passionate embrace, not that Mike was really trying, as gently as possible, to extricate himself from Anna's determined advances.

There are times when people have a tendency to believe the worst, even against all logic, for Jillian, this was one. All she wanted, at that moment, was to be somewhere else. In her rush to get away, she struck the tray against the door post scattering its contents and breaking the crockery. Mike and Anna, both responded to the noise. Mike seized the opportunity to break free. When she pressed her 'attack', Mike grabbed Anna's arms and pinned her against the bookshelf. As kindly as he could, against his mounting wrath, Mike pleaded, "Give it up, enough already. This is not going to work."

He looked deep into her eyes. That this had been an ordeal for her was obvious. He saw the look of defeat come into her face as she shrank in upon herself. She was no longer the 'temptress' that she had tried to be. Anna was, if possible, even more naked than she was before, emotionally and spiritually, as well as physically. She ran from the room, crying, scooping up her cloak as she ran. The girl ran along the corridor and ducked into the first unoccupied side corridor she came upon.

Mike felt sorry for her, and under any other circumstances, would have followed her to try and help, but that would have to wait. First, he had to find Jill. If she had assumed the worst then, no doubt she was feeling very betrayed and hurt. As he ran through the various corridors looking for her, his concern made him think of the Gillian back home, how, if she was anything like Jill, she must surely have been terribly hurt by "the great Mike Colford". More and more, Mike wanted to wrap things up here so that he could get back to her and hopefully set things right, if that was possible.

"You don't have to wait," Max told him. *"I am tied in to all the complex's communication lines. You may not have direct voice access, but you can talk with her through me."*

"But would she even want to hear from me?"

"I believe so. You see, I have taken a few liberties in the past couple of days, during your down time. I think that she will be very glad to hear from you directly."

"Now that is what I call a great 'wife.'", Mike quipped, *"One that even helps you patch things up with your girlfriend. Now if only I could find Jill..."*

No sooner was the thought complete when he turned a corner and nearly ran headlong into her. Jillian's eyes were red and puffy. What she had been doing was obvious. What was also apparent was that she didn't want to see Mike, she turned to flee in the opposite direction.

"Wait," Mike called, half a plea, half a command, "please."

Jillian froze mid-stride and turned to face him. She was hurt, but she was also very angry. "Why should I? What was all that crap you fed me about another Gillian back home? What's wrong, aren't we young enough for you? You seem to like children better."

"It's not like that," Mike countered. "She was doing what you tried to do, only, she was much less subtle and much more persistent. Didn't you see her robe on the floor?"

Jillian had, only now did the significance of the pile on the floor seem obvious to her. But she was not completely convinced. "You didn't seem to be minding her persistence, too much."

"I was trying to fight her off without hurting her. If I was enjoying it so much, how come I am not still back there? Why is that kid somewhere, probably hiding, crying her eyes out too?"

"Why? What did you do, hit her?"

"No, I didn't hit her," Mike snapped back, angry now. How could she be so thick? Yet, he understood. She was hurt and speaking out of her pain. Working to get himself under control he tried to be gentle. Dealing honestly with emotionally injured women was something very new to him. He found that it was important to him that Jillian understand, and he knew, too, that she would be able to aid him in helping the young girl, who was also seriously wounded, by this incident. The 'bosses' he would deal with himself, later.

"Look, Jillian, it is important that you believe me. She was just a kid sent by an overzealous bastard to do a job no girl or woman should be asked to do for 'king', 'country' or 'God'."

"Maybe," she said, uncertain, "I gotta think. I'll talk to

you later."

Later never came. That afternoon other groups arrived. More sane and reasonable people, Christians called the "Peter and Paul Community" – as near as Mike could figure, they were an analog to his own Roman Catholic church, also a number of Buddhist groups. Both groups accepted him readily, and they were excited about the idea of ultimately securing their freedom by offering new, seemingly miraculous, forms of healing. Most of the afternoon had been taken up with showing them around the medical center. They were suitably impressed, but as Max had told him, the desktop terminal fascinated them most of all.

"That is absolutely amazing," remarked Ahmet, one of the leaders. "We never thought that this was possible. All data processing is handled by the government. All technical knowledge is classified 'Top Secret'."

"But what about business?" Mike asked. "The library described a well-developed system of private industry, and what I saw in the city suggested an industrial level equal to my world's late 20th century. By that time, on my world, almost all businesses had their own systems in place."

"Not here. All companies are serviced by the Ministry of Information Processing. That keeps control of all data handling tightly in government hands with the added advantage of allowing the government to keep extremely close tabs on all companies. That control is unbelievable!"

"But that also means that they wouldn't expect anyone outside of the Ministry to have any knowledge of computers;

which is a great advantage to us."

"Do you know a lot about computers?" Ahmet asked.

"You might say that I've got one in my head," Mike quipped, and then left it at that, leaving Ahmet with a slightly puzzled look on his face. He was counting on Max rather heavily to be able to help him crack the government computer. His plan was starting to come together nicely.

The afternoon had been most helpful to Mike. If the government kept such a close control on all automated processing, then no one would question anything that those top secret machines produced. Their security systems were all based on magnetic identity cards, controlled by those same central computers. If Mike could get in to those computers ahead of time, he and Max could enter a list of security id's. He could reproduce the necessary credentials on one of his own lab's terminals. The 3-D printer in the OR could reproduce insignia of the Imperial Security forces assigned to the Emperor himself.

They could all walk straight in, past the defense systems, without challenge. It all just might work. He was sure that the central computer could provide him with floor plans of the capital's key buildings, and the location of all the strategic points that he would need to disable or control. He went over the possibilities in his mind as he lay back on his bed. It was really taking shape.

"Good plan," Max commented *"about as good as it can get, for now. Best time to turn to other things, don't you think? Gillian is standing by at her terminal, waiting to hear from you.*

She tells me that she has been very worried about all of this."

All of a sudden Mike was lost. *"What do I do?* he asked Max. Butterflies were churning around in his stomach and his mouth went dry. It was a good thing that he didn't have to actually speak to her. He didn't think that he could manage it. He swung his feet over the side of the bed bringing, himself into a sitting position.

"Just talk as if you were talking to me," Max instructed. *"If you want I can patch you through an unmonitored circuit, essentially, 'step out of the room'. But if I did that I also wouldn't be able to keep others from listening in."*

"No, it's OK, Max. You know it all anyway...

Hello, Gillian... " he began.

"Hello, Mike," It was Gillian's voice. Had Max simulated it in his head, or was he hearing it because he knew the sound of her voice? As they talked, Mike wondered if Max could do the same with his voice at the other end for Gillian, or was she reading his words off a terminal screen. In any event, it was great to finally begin to say the things that should have been said a long time ago.

"Gillian," Mike faltered, at a loss for words, *"I don't know another way of saying it, but straight out – I love you..."*

"I know", Gillian answered, *"I think I've known from the very beginning. Something clicked that first night. That's what made the time since so very hard."*

"I think I know what you mean. The more I ran away

from the truth, the harder it became. But I kept running because I was afraid that you might only be in love with my image. At least that's what I told myself. I used it as an excuse to evade the real truth: I love you, and there will never be anyone else ever again. I was petrified of being trapped."

"And now?" Gillian asked.

Mike thought he could hear the tremor in her voice.

"If Rob Gauthier was right about me being the last of the Lothario's, then the breed is now officially extinct. Even if you tell me now that you never want to see me again, you are, and will always be, the only woman for me."

"Then we'll hang up a wreath when you get home. Just so long as you come back to me. I love you, Mike. I've waited this long, and I'll keep on waiting."

They 'talked' for over an hour before Max told Mike that he heard sounds in the hall outside his room. Mike said a quick good-bye to Gillian on a pretext that he hoped would not cause her concern. If Max's replication of her voice (if that is what it was) was accurate, she already sounded worried enough.

Mike shut off the light, and drew his pistol from his jacket. After the morning's experience, Mike had a very good idea how 'unsubtle' the Zealots could be. He dropped to a crouch by the door, between the end of the bed and the wall. There was another pause in the corridor, and then the curtain that served as a door was pushed aside hesitantly. Mike held his place, in the deepest shadow. His visitors, there were two, carried no lights. Mike's eyes were adapting quickly, too quickly to be natural, bless Max. The shapes crept towards the bed. One was smaller than the other, though both were small. They moved quietly, but didn't seem to be trying to sneak up on him. Their hands were empty. Finally one of them spoke.

"Mike, are you still awake?" It was Jillian. It was a bit disorienting for Mike – after just saying good-bye to Gillian.

"You can turn on the lamp," he said, rising from his position of concealment. She did, and Mike had to shield his over sensitive eyes, for a moment, while Max re-adjusted things inside his visual cortex.

Beside Jill, Anna, already hesitant, backed off even more at the sight of the weapon in Mike's hand. When he saw the girl's discomfort, he put the gun away, and gave her his most disarming smile.

"Sorry, but I wasn't sure if maybe Marek hadn't sent more of your people with a more direct mission," he explained.

"They aren't my people anymore," Anna answered. "Not after this morning, I can't believe them any longer, especially when I see how people of this community live. At home we live like trapped animals, always on the run, never trusting anyone. Everyone looks out for him or herself first. That is, unless Marek or one of the 'prophets' has a special job for you – then it's your mission to serve God and the community. The 'Peter and Paul' community said that I can join them, so did the 'Jerusalem in Exile' people that arrived late this afternoon."

"I'll bet Marek and his bunch had something to say when they heard that."

"They aren't talking to anyone," Jillian told him. "After we talked this morning I went looking for Anna. As you can see, I found her. She was overwrought. Both because she had failed in her 'appointed mission' and because of what the mission had required. It was all I could do to get her to come and see Ezra. He was beautiful, as always."

"He really was," Anna added. "We talked for hours and hours. He talked to me of God in ways that our teachers never did, as a loving and caring God. He surprised me when he talked of Jesus. He said that he didn't believe in him as Christians did, but he spoke of him as a peacemaker, with great sorrow for what a few misguided, overly-political, people had done so long ago. He made me understand that there is a difference between when a person is led to commit a bad act, and the kind of person it is who commits the act; that even good people, sometimes, make mistakes. The more he talked to me, the more I felt his belief in me as a good person. All we ever got at home was that we were all depraved, and could only do bad, and that only missions for God were good and would save us."

As the young girl talked, Mike felt the great pain that she had suffered in that negative atmosphere, all her life. He felt his anger, toward the people who had done this to her, growing once again.

"Then Marcus joined us, I don't know how he knew to, he's a Magdalene brother you know. They teach the mercy of God. They have sisters too. He says that I can stay with the sisters for as long as I want to. They'll help me find a place in the larger community, when I am ready. We're all going to be very busy preparing to implement your plan when it's ready, he tells me, so I wanted to come and apologize to you tonight and to say thank you...," her voice trailed off, as she remembered what she was apologizing for.

Mike reached out and enfolded her in his arms. *'She is so tiny'*, he thought. He also surprised himself by the depth of his paternal feelings toward her. For a moment, he cradled her gently like a fragile and precious object, making (what he hoped were) soothing sounds. When he released her, Anna stood on her tip toes and kissed him on the cheek and hurried out of the room. Mike watched her go and then turned towards Jillian.

"You were really great with her, even this morning, or so she says," then she kissed Mike on the other cheek. "I'm sorry, too. Especially because, if I hadn't over reacted this morning, I might have been more help."

"And what about Marek and the others? They won't appreciate our subversion of their operative. They can make all kinds of trouble."

"Not anymore..," Jillian announced, with a slight touch of glee. "... Dad has had them locked up - for corrupting a minor, among other things. The conventions governing our communities state that any visitors or delegations from outside have to obey our laws. Despite her age she really is only a child. Dad and the others on the council were incensed when they heard what the Zealots told her to do. Marek and his party are locked up, but the message that we sent their people is that they are making a reconnaissance, and will be unavailable until the operation is over. By then it will be too late for them to hurt us."

"Never assume that," Mike told her, "Fanatics are always dangerous. Your only hope is that there are enough people in their group feeling the same pressure as Anna. Because if there are, then their group will not survive once freedom is attained."

"We'll remember that," she promised, "Now, we both need to get some sleep. I'll see you in the morning." Giving him a parting kiss on the cheek, she left.

"Well, buddy..," he said to Max, *"This day seems to be ending alright, good night."* As he talked to Max, Mike shucked off his clothes, and letting them fall where they would, he rolled into bed. Bed had never felt so good. For only a few more moments, he reviewed his 'reunion' with Gillian, courtesy of Max, and then fell into a deep, natural sleep without the help of his partner. Of course, Max stood guard.

The next morning, Mike arose fresh Crawling back into the clothes he had left on the cold stone floor, he wished that he had been a little more farsighted. He made a note to get his spare clothes from his office cupboard. He thanked his wayward ways for the fact that he actually kept spare clothes, both civvies and uniforms, in both his office and lab. He made his way around to the main hall, not surprised to find everyone in morning meditation. To his surprise, though, a table had been added to the far end of the room and on it were the vessels which he would normally have associated with what, back home, would be called a Catholic Mass. Behind the table, sat Brother Marcus, next to a younger man from the Peter and Paul community. The younger man was wearing a shawl or stole of some kind about his shoulders. Mike looked about. He found Sam, Aaron, Jillian, and Ezra, in fact, the whole Jewish community was there as well. He was a bit perplexed, particularly when as the meditation finished the young man next to Brother Marcus rose and dismissed the gathering with a Christian blessing.

Over breakfast Jillian explained. "As a sign of our solidarity, they share our visible prayer and we share theirs. Obviously, a Christian Eucharist does not have the same meaning for us, and our prayers do not have exactly the same meaning for the Christians. There is one meeting point though, the silence of meditation. In mediation, each person meets God in his or her own way, but we recognize that it is the same God. We may never reconcile the differences in how we express our faith, but we share the common factor of our experience of it at the deepest level."

Mike was floored. Wait till he spoke to Gillian again that night. *"Won't she be surprised,"* he thought, *"or will she?"*

For the rest of the day, Mike was busy explaining the idea, that he had come up with, to Aaron, Sam and, most importantly, to Ezra. It was, he believed, simplicity itself. In just over seven weeks' time, the full Senate was due to convene in New Rome in Imperial Session (which Max had told him seemed to be right where Washington D.C. should be). The

Emperor always presided over the assembly, himself. All the regional governors and their staff were required to attend the opening session.

That also meant a lot of new faces about the Capital. Security people would be relying totally on the magnetic passes. So, about a week or less, before the session convened, he would take the Hellbat in, on stealth mode, carrying a full complement of six people. Most of the team would remain with the bird to ensure their escape. It meant taking a risk that they might have to engage capital guards, but it couldn't be helped. To Mike's surprise, Ezra didn't object.

"We risk a small evil," he said, "and pray that God will protect us from it, so that we may achieve a greater good."

Once in the capital, Brother Marcus, from the Peter and Paul Community, who, Mike had learned, had been an officer in the Imperial Guard before his conversion would guide him through Ministry of Information Processing and help him bypass their security measures.

"Only those who know the system know where the holes in it are," he told Mike. "The brass is so positive that no one outside the guard knows about these weaknesses, that they haven't gone to the expense of patching them up."

"But you know them, and they know that you used to be one of them," Mike pointed out.

"And as far as they know, I'm dead. When I learned the truth that the brethren were teaching I volunteered to do a reconnaissance mission for my commander, from which I never intended to return. My blood stained hat and torn tunic were found, as I had intended, just outside the city. The signs that I left suggested that my 'body' had been dumped in the river you call the Potomac. They never bothered to look for it, which was all the better for me then, and for us now."

If Marcus was right, Mike should have no trouble accessing the main computer and cracking the system's passwords. With proper backup and a little luck, the rest would be history, a new history. In the meantime, there were many preparations to be made. Everyone involved had to be trained to use the new weaponry properly, or in spite of all the best intentions, too many people would be hurt. They also had to learn where to go and what positions would be most useful. In many ways, Brother Marcus proved invaluable. Lastly, they just needed to be trained, physically, to ensure that they were fit enough for the rigors of the plan.

At the same time, Mike was training as many others as he could to use the computer terminals in the Med Center. He was pleased to see how easily the physicians of the various communities readily learned the new techniques. It would be a while before they would master them, and there was still a large body of anatomical theory, epidemiology and pharmacology to be assimilated and, in some cases, to be adapted to account for variances in this dimension's evolution.

Through it all Jill, was his right hand. Once he had begun to get it together with Gillian back home, he found that he was able to relax around Jill, and they soon had become fast friends – a real first for Mike Colford. As the day of his mission to the capital approached, however, he sensed that she was becoming apprehensive. So was Gillian back home. It was understandable, but he didn't know how to deal with it. In the end, he had no alternative but to try and put it out of his mind, or it would distract him during the mission. That would be disastrous. Mike was forced to conclude, that it was one of the few positives of his former lifestyle. He never before had anyone else to worry about when he stepped onto a launch platform, or (now) into a shift chamber.

The evening before his flight to the capital, he found himself alone after dinner, which was odd. Usually, Jill or both Jill and Anna would seek him out to talk; often about some detail of the new medical techniques that they were learning. Both had opted to be in the first wave of trainees. But tonight they were nowhere to be seen. So Mike took the time to return to his old office in the Med. Center, to put the finishing touches on a program that would allow for the transfer of medical information to the computers on the government system, as soon as control of those machines was firmly in the hands of this populous.

As he entered the building and rounded the corner, he saw the light on in his office. Sure that he had turned it off when he last left, Mike was immediately on the defensive. Cautiously, he crept down the hall with his back pressed against the wall. *"I'm getting too good at the cloak and dagger stuff..,"* he thought, *"...and getting too jumpy,"* he added, when it turned out only to be Jillian working in the outer office. Mike felt a little foolish.

"Better a little foolish...," Max suggested, leaving the sentence unfinished.

"True enough, Partner."

Jillian looked up, with a start, as Mike entered the office.

"I didn't hear you come in," she said, and Mike flushed thinking again of how foolish it now seemed. He told Jill of what he called his overreaction, but she agreed with Max.

"You can never be too careful. You remember your first night with us."

It wasn't that long ago, but it seemed to Mike like an age.

"You know," she went on, "you never did tell me how you came to be your world's first inter-dimensional traveler. Or, how it happens that a man of you convictions about peace and human rights should be a soldier."

"There's really not much to tell," Mike began. "Since the end of the 20th Century, in my world, the number of people finishing high school and wanting to go on to higher education has climbed to over eighty percent. That is far more than the world's network of universities can handle. To meet the need a massive worldwide restructuring of the system became necessary. First, each country established an expanded network of community colleges, where a bachelor's degree or technical equivalent was the terminal degree. If you went to one of those institutions, that was as far as you went in any given discipline, formally. The universities of the world formed an admissions network, where all persons who met the academic standard for admission, participated in an entrance lottery, only it wasn't long before the rich and powerful found ways to subvert the process.

"Qualified applicants were given six tries at winning admission. If, on the sixth try, the applicant was still not selected then that person had to accept that a community college education was all they would have."

"And that was it? What happens to those exceptionally gifted people, who might not be lucky enough to win the lottery?"

"Well, the community colleges were not always the end of it. If an individual was recognized as outstanding in their field, they might be granted academic recognition for their accomplishments, and admitted to university. But that takes a few years. Also, if you already had some kind of body of work behind you to show an exceptional talent in your chosen field, then you might be able to get an exemption after your sixth miss, but even that was very difficult due to the corruption of the system. But, as you might have guessed, I didn't have the connections. So I was never "recognized". Some of my friends say it's because I'm too eclectic, my detractors say it's because I'm a 'scatter-brain'. Whichever it is, I'm interested in a little bit of everything, and a lot of certain specific things, and too impatient to wait to be recognized in any of them."

"But didn't you tell me that you started what you call college at eleven years of age?" Jill asked.

"That's right. But it only shows how corrupt the system was. Under the old system, I would have had university acceptance in any one of my chosen fields."

"So this is where the military came in?"

"That's right. Each school had to hold a certain number of places, in various disciplines, for members of the military. I knew that my IQ tests would qualify me for any program that they were offering, so I signed on the dotted line. My original plan was to get a Ph.D. on the military's ticket, do the required ten year hitch, and then retire to a civilian position at some university where I would teach, do research and continue to learn. I figured that I could handle it. We were at peace, mostly. Things were fairly stable, and the university time was counted towards the mandatory hitch, if you worked on military projects during the summer."

"Obviously, your plan worked," Jill observed.

"Not exactly as planned…" Mike said, "We have an expression, 'Life had other plans…'" He went on to tell her of his father's death and his flight into the military with the help of his "uncles".

"Well, as far as my original plan went, I was right about a lot of things. One, I aced the IQ tests. They said that I was a super-genius, which most everybody knew already. Two, I was in university within a few weeks of completing basic training, doing a degree in particle physics, at an accelerated rate. Three, it was possible for me to work the summers for Uncle Sam, the military, that is, and still do some summer school. Then one day, while I was putting the finishing touches on my master's thesis, just by luck, I was chitchatting with a young surgeon doing research in bionic limb replacement. He was having some problems that I was able to help him with, and before long I was hooked. I studied medicine on my own, with the blessing of the school. By the time I graduated with a PhD, I was ready to do a medical residency. ”

"But how did a physicist-doctor become an inter-dimensional traveller?" Jillian asked.

"That's comes out of a combination of my love for adventure and the politics of the Pentagon," He told her. Mike went on to tell her of his adventures in space and about the old Generals in Washington that didn't care about his degrees, just that he was the best pilot they had seen in years, who they wanted flying missions and testing weapons.

"So I guess that you really regret coming here?" Jillian asked. "I mean, here you are planning to lead a combat mission – a mission that you conceived."

"No, I have no regrets. I've learned so much about myself, and about life, in the past few weeks since this adventure began. I have spent most of my life in a test tube. I know a lot about the processes that make things work, but almost nothing about the way the real life works. More importantly, I have learned that life is not just "there", as something for me to study. I have to be a part of it, and to live for something, someone beyond myself. You and your people have taught me more in the past few weeks, than eight years of solid academia ever could." Mike smiled at Jill, as he heard the truth in his own words; and she returned his smile.

"I said it before..," she told him, earnestly, "... if the Gillian you left behind doesn't want you when you get back, I'll be waiting. What's more, if this works, then thanks to you, we won't be living as fugitives anymore."

Mike just smiled. He couldn't bring himself to tell her about his nightly conversations with Gillian, even if he could find a way of explaining Max, the living computer.

In the remaining time before the convening Imperial Session, Mike found himself working longer and longer days, overseeing the training of the 'troops' that would seize the capital, while at the same time giving lectures and workshops to those who had dived head long into the CATS programs They now found themselves in a world of wonders they never thought possible; one that was often very difficult to understand. They were definitely motivated but, often had to take, on faith, the operations of various diagnostic and therapeutic machines. It was a good thing that faith was something of which they had an abundant supply. Their part was more important than that of the 'shock troops'. It was this knowledge that made them valuable. It would secure their position. Without it, they might hold onto power in the capital for a few months, or even a few years, until some remnant of one of the old regimes thought the time was right. Then, they would fall, and all that they brought with them in technology would belong to the new tyrants to use or not use as they wished. This could only be prevented if the population supported their new government.

"The real revolution begins with a revolutionary new medical technology," Mike told the assembled leaders, "...but it doesn't stop there. It mustn't stop there. So long as the government rules from within a tight, restrictive core of power, it is vulnerable to the exact same kind of coup we are going to pull off in a few days from now. It doesn't make any difference if you're a benevolent dictator or a despotic one. Only real freedom lasts.

"My world's history is full of examples of governments, and rulers who conquered vast territories and ruled as absolute monarchs. In my world they all eventually fell, giving way to democracy. The first, most important areas you must address are freedom of expression and freedom of information, including a free press. If the people are kept aware of what's going on, they'll support you. If somebody tries to take their new freedoms away from them again, they will rally behind you. You have a wealth of new knowledge in the computer banks here. In the capital you may find more information that the government never told you about, hidden away in their computers. That's the real power in the secular world. Your faith, and your fidelity to it, I have learned, will keep you going; knowledge will keep your government going."

"Will you stay on with us, afterward?" someone asked.

"No," Mike replied, honestly. "I'm no avatar. You have your own wisdom and your own counsel to guide you. I have never known a more balanced society. And, this is your world. Besides," he added with a grin, "there are other dimensions for me to visit."

That day, the meeting ended on a high note. Mike was pleased with the level of their morale. Confidence was everything in an operation of this kind. Even the best trained squad is of very little use, if they try walking past check points with knocking knees and sweaty armpits. They still had a lot to do in a short time, but Mike was hopeful.

Mike was unaware, however, of how close he was to being either pulled home against his will, or abandoned where he was. For back at *Project Symphony*, Senator Reall had returned with some big brass from the Pentagon. This time, he was determined that the General would not be able to face him down and get away with it.

"Damn it, man..." he yelled, "I have proof that that machine has been transmitting information to someone on the base, outside of the control complex. Now there's nothing in the mission description or specifications that accounts for this. What's more, it is using a dad blasted secure channel unlike anyone has ever seen before. My people have used the most sophisticated monitoring equipment the CIA, the NSA, the KGB or the FSB could come up with, but the damn machine foiled them all. Now I've had it! Either that abomination reveals the contents of those communications, or you are going to pull its plug. We'll bring Colford back using the Twin Pines AI, if we can. If we can't, well he knew the risks."

Briefly, James Urnbreach felt like he was a cadet at the Air Force Academy again. The two four-star generals Reall brought with him sat there stone faced, but their presence said it all. As far as they were concerned, this came from the top and Reall was sitting on the right hand of God. Sitting beside the General, Maureen allowed her hand to softly brush his under the table. He leaned closer to her, and she whispered in his ear.

"However you want to play it, we're behind you, all of us." She looked around the table at the engineers and section heads assembled, and at Mitch Craig, sitting opposite. Everyone was confident that the "old war horse" wouldn't let them down. And, damn, he wasn't about to either!

For a long moment he said nothing, then in a most emphatic tone, looking Reall straight in the eye and emphasizing each individual word he said simply...

"Go-To-Hell!"

Sitting there as he was, puffed up like a peacock, that was the last response that the senator expected. He started to rise from his seat red faced and sputtering with rage, when General Wolf gently placed a hand on his shoulder. Wolf was a towering hulk of a man who often used his height to intimidate subordinates.

"It's OK, Jan," he said, rising from his chair, "leave this to me." Then turning to Urnbreach he said, "Now, Jim, I really don't think you understand the gravity of this situation. We, General Rulph and I that is, support Senator Reall and I am sure that we speak for the Old Man in this..."

"I'm sure you do," General Urnbreach responded sarcastically, "Now let me tell you a thing or two, *Pinkie*. For one thing, ever since it was discovered that this was where the base's arsenal turned up, the Old Man has been in constant touch. As per regulations, if you ever bothered to read the manual, boy, once American weapons became involved in this operation, as senior military officer I must report directly to the 'C-in-C', daily."

"I would remind you," 'Pinkie' cut in, "that we two

---

have the authority to replace you as the senior officer on base and on the Project."

"You most certainly do, but then I would be required to file a final report. That report would, of course, have to contain any reservations that I might have about my replacement or replacements, and then I might feel constrained to explain in detail how you got that *Purple Heart* in Libya. Pinkie, you're an asshole. You were an asshole when I was just a plebe and you were cadet captain. You were an asshole when you were a squadron leader. You were an even bigger asshole when you made flight commander. And now, you're fast reaching the highest heights of assholedom. You really don't want to motivate me to do something about that. In fact, after this little 'Hi how are ya' you might actually want to give some serious thoughts to retirement. Only you and I know how you came to be injured in that particular way." He left the implied threat hanging.

Caught up short by Jim Urnbreach's speech, General Wolf sputtered and fumed for an instant and, then slowly retook his seat, but that wasn't to be the end of it. It was evident that General Rulph was not going to sit idly by while his colleague was so soundly lambasted by an underling. Just as he was about to open his mouth "the old warhorse" rounded on him.

"And what about you, Freddy? Should I include that little hundred-and-twenty-proof confession of yours, the one that you made to me in the O-Club a few years ago? About how, when you were last on Presidential detail, you managed to lose the 'football' and faked it for over an hour by carrying around a spare brief case with a presidential seal hastily stuck on its side. You know that it doesn't matter that the damn thing has been deactivated for more than twenty five years. This president still thinks that it's good "PR" for the few remaining hawks among the voters. You should have come clean back then."

Then, to his surprise, although a little more subdued, Rulph pressed on.

"I did," he told Urnbreach, "So you really don't have anything on me, Jimmy, do you? And the order still stands. I want whoever this machine is feeding information to found, arrested, and silenced. I want the operation turned over to the back-up facility and I want that 'THING' shut down. And I want it NOW!"

"Actually, I can tell you with whom Max has been communicating." It was Dr. Gauthier at the end of the table. "You see, when the base disappeared with Colonel Colford, very few buildings were left untouched. My home, thankfully, was one of them. Since that time, I have had a house guest, my nurse, Ms. Green. Quite an advantageous arrangement, really, we've never gotten so much work done." He smiled at the assembled generals. "But to the point: You see, Mike Colford and my nurse, it seems, have grown quite attached to each other. It took quite a bit for either of them to admit it at first, so things got off to a rocky start. Over the past few weeks, Max has been acting as a medium of communication between them, while Colford is away. Well, as you know, or should know, if you've read our reports, Max does not reveal the contents of Colonel Colford's personal communications unless they have direct bearing on the mission. This certainly does not, or as Max might say these days: 'It's none of your damn business.'"

General Rulph was taken aback by the doctor's report.

"You're sure of this?"

"Very, Max uses my computer to communicate with Ms. Green. The voice that comes out of the speaker is Mike Colford's, (a good simulation, too). What's more, Gillian, Nurse Green that is, has shared parts of the communications with me. She has become a close friend, you see, and of course the Colonel is my godson."

"So, this whole supposed security breach is nothing more than lovers whispering 'sweet nothings'?" Rulph asked, turning on Reall. "For this we came all the way up here from Washington, Reall? Love talk!?" Then turning to General Urnbreach, "Well, I guess, Jim, we have nothing to report to the Old Man after all, do we?"

"Perhaps not," Urnbreach replied, "by the way do say 'hi' to Rick Belton when you get back. I understand that he's a full bird-colonel now." Then leaning closer, so that only Rulph could hear, "It's funny how homophobic the military continues to be, even today, isn't it?" Then, so the assembled group could hear. "Have a good trip back, Freddy," he added grinning broadly. The general hated blackmail, it was a poor defense against those types, but when the only defense you have against a gang of bullies is a stick with a rusty nail in it, you don't throw it away.

That evening, Gillian waited by the terminal earlier

than usual. Other nights, it wasn't until nearly ten o'clock or later before Mike could get away from the others. He was working so hard. She was really worried. Not only that, but there was something that everyone seemed to be hiding from her. She didn't know what it was, and hadn't dared to bring it up with Mike, because she was equally afraid of knowing the answer. She knew that Mike would tell her if she asked. Tonight, Gillian had decided, she had to ask. After the day's events with Senator Reall and the Pentagon brass, she felt that she couldn't put it off. Gillian looked at her watch. It was just turning eight thirty. As arranged, Max came on line.

"Good evening, Gillian," he said in his own 'voice', then without further preamble she heard the simulation of Mike's voice.

"Hello, Love."

Gillian always marvelled at how Max could, ever so perfectly, produce the proper inflection. But tonight she almost wished he didn't. She could hear a worried tone in Mike's voice that she didn't like.

"I have something to tell you," he continued, "I have been putting it off, but I can't any longer, 'cause it's happening tonight."

"Here it comes," Gillian thought, fighting the urge to bite her finger nails like she did as a child.

Mike went on to tell her of his plan to fly into the capital that night, and to break into the government's computer facility. He did his best to downplay the danger, explaining to her the details that he had learned from Brother Marcus about the holes in the security system, and how he would go about making the best of them. Of course, there was really nothing that he could say that would allay her fears. In the end, he had to promise to let Max transmit all the details of the mission as they unfolded back to the control complex. Gillian would be waiting there, in front of the computer, listening to each and every step he took until he was safely out of harm's way again.

Mike knew he had to accept that. He had made a choice. Gillian was a major part of his life now. She would worry, and there was nothing that he could do but try his best not to take unnecessary risks.

After he broke contact Mike left his room for the rear exit where the Hellbat was waiting. There beside it, stood his crew, restless and wanting to be underway. They had almost as difficult a task as did Mike. If they were discovered, they would have to use their weapons. It was an extremely difficult prospect for them to face. The alternative, however, was the Hellbat and its weapons possibly falling into government hands, and the disastrous repercussions that would follow.

There were silent nods, but no one said anything as Mike approached. After one last check of their equipment, they boarded the helicopter. Just as Mike was about to take his place in the pilot's seat, he noticed Jill standing in the shadows. He knew how difficult this must be for her, too. Unlike her counterpart back home, she had known about tonight's mission for the last eight weeks. Now that the moment had arrived, she had to wait here, without the advantage Mike's interface to keep her abreast of things. Mike didn't know what to do, but Max came up with something.

"She knows how to monitor telemetry," he said *"feed the Hellbat's onboard telemetry through the pulse-transmitter/scrambler and then piggy back the return signal on a government carrier wave. The powers-that-be will never suspect, and folks back here can be kept up-to-date from the Med Centre's console..."*

"Very creative suggestion," Mike commented, *"can you set it up?"*

"I can, and it is all ready to go" Max told him.

The process was quite simple, just a matter of a little extra programming entered into one of the Hellbat transmitter's pre-processors, and they were ready to get underway. After a last minute equipment check Mike fired up the helicopter's engine.

It was full dark as he lifted. To their advantage, the night was cloudy and moonless. Flying at Mach 3 in full stealth mode, Mike turned south towards the capital.

"It shouldn't be too hard to find," he told Max, *"it's right where DC should be."*

After they had been airborne a few moments, Gabe, the large young man whom he had first encountered on that first night, and who was now flying in the co-pilot's seat, keyed the intercom mic on his helmet.

"Colonel Mike, please explain it to me again. This craft

is making a heck of a lot of noise, how can it sneak right past New Rome like you say?"

One day, Mike had found Gabe playing with the mini CATS system built into the Hellbat; a sort of on-board simulator. It turned out that he was a natural pilot, much like Mike himself. Mike decided that, in the time left, he might be able to teach Gabe how to fly. His training was now almost complete, but there were still questions that Mike had very little time to cover. He gave his large friend a smile:

"The noise you hear is only inside," Mike told him. "The helicopter projects a sonic field around itself that suppresses, dampens and then eliminates all noise. From only a few inches away, this bird is silent as a... church." Mike almost said 'silent as a tomb', but checked himself at the last minute.

"It would do no good to introduce negative imagery at this point," Max agreed.

For a while they flew on in silence, when they were nearing New Rome/Washington, Brother Marcus, at the tactical station, activated his intercom. It seemed strange to Mike that a religious man should have elected to join this mission. Brother Marcus volunteered, on the condition that he remained a non-combatant, arguing that he would be the only one capable of leading Mike through the Ministry of Information Processing.

"OK," he said, "Mike, let's review our plan."

"Right!" Mike replied. "First, we approach by following the river bypassing the capital center and over to the Ministry.

We then land inside the apex of the of the building's interior court, where all the offices should be vacant at this time."

The similarity of Marcus' sketch of the Ministry building to the Pentagon, back home, surprised Mike; even to its location at point analogous to the Pentagon's in Virginia. At first, he thought it odd to have so obvious a parallel in landmarks with such different functions, until Marcus informed him that 'Defense' was a function of the Ministry of Information Processing, one of its prime functions. It made sense to the Emperor to have the military and the Ministry of Information operating out of the same location.

"Remember, when we are flying over the capital; don't get too close to the 'Gods of Fertility' monument. It is always very well lighted. We would be visible for miles. You were briefed on its appearance?"

"Sort of..," was all Mike could say. It had struck Mike as odd that everyone could give him a reasonably good description of the monument in terms of height and width, but no one wanted to draw him a picture, not even Marcus, who was very familiar with the structure. But since New Rome had a very close facsimile of the Pentagon and he White House, Mike had a pretty good guess what to expect.

Good guess or no, Mike was still taken aback as New Rome came into view in the distance. It was not a reasonable facsimile or a close copy. Apart from a few distinctly Roman additions, this was the DC that he knew well. The names, and at times purpose, of the buildings might be different, but he could have found his way around without any problems.

At this point all his skill as a pilot was required as he brought his stealth helicopter over the city just above the house tops. Then, just prior to the capital buildings, he turned off toward the Pentagon/Ministry approaching from the 'base' of the pentagonal structure. Mike practically glided the bird to a stop in the shadow of the apex. Marcus was right. There were no security lights inside the yard. Sensors that would be triggered by the magnetic fields of aircar motors were in place, but nothing that could have detected the Hellbat.

There were no office lights near their landing site, so on the ground, the helicopter was enfolded in darkness. The squad took up positions just inside the perimeter of shadow, while Marcus and Mike stripped off their flight gear to reveal fairly convincing versions of the security force uniform. Both wore insignia of sufficient rank to keep them from being overruled by a stray junior officer, but not so high up as to raise questions as to why two members of the brass should be there so late.

They shouldn't have problems, Marcus assured Mike, because at this time of the year each regional governor sends his own brass on ahead to make special security arrangements. Old Rome may have fallen, but New Rome was just as sinister when it came to advancement by assassination. Those who held power were appropriately paranoid, Mike concluded (and was seconded by Max).

The pair followed the wall along the western edge of the apex of the structure until they found a door. It was locked, even though no one really expected anyone to be able to enter from the inside of the structure. That was one of those weaknesses Brother Marcus had told him about. As they approached the door the plan hit a snag. On the door that Marcus told him would have a lock that would be easy to pick, there was a now a keypad lock, possibly tied into an alarm.

Mike looked at Marcus, then back at the lock. They needed to get past the lock or the mission and the "revolution" was a failure. He thought for a moment, and then turned back to Marcus. "How often do you think the combination would be changed?" he asked.

Marcus shrugged. "Why would they have to change the combination?"

That was enough for Mike. If that was how Marcus saw it, then it was probable that the powers-that-be here thought the same way. He asked Max to enhance his vision to the maximum. He examined the security pad from the top, and then from all possible sides, then Max said, *"9-2-4-7-3"*. Mike entered the numbers.

Marcus stopped dead. "How did you do that? How could you know that code?" His hand dropped to the weapon on his belt.

"Let's just say that my vision has been enhanced by my technology. My enhanced vision allows me to see what others can't. If you could look very closely enough at the pad, you would be able to discern which numbers are more worn than others. Obviously, since they don't expect an incursion from this side of the building, they think like you. They never change the code."

Marcus relaxed a bit, but his body language betrayed a

residual tension. "How did you know the order to press?"

"There we got lucky, really. My guess is that the people who use that door don't see why it needs such an elaborate lock. They don't take care when they press the buttons. Their hands slide over the keys, from one to the next. Those minute wear patterns I told you about, they are directional. You can tell where they start and end from the edges," Mike explained as Max relayed the information to him.

Marcus relaxed and they entered the building.

Without the need for light, Mike led Marcus through an inner and then outer office. Once in the lighted corridor, Marcus took the lead as they wended their way through a series of twists and turns.

"I hope you're keeping track of all this, buddy," Mike said to Max. *"'...cause if something happens and I have to get out alone..,"* Mike left the thought unfinished.

"Semper fidelis," Max replied.

After what felt like an eternity, they arrived in the intended corridor. Attached to the frame of a large door was an ancient looking keypad.

"As I told you," Marcus said, "we have to enter a security pass-code... and this code they do change often."

But Mike had long since assured him that so 'ancient' a security system presented very little problem. Now he was true to his word. From his tool kit, he produced a miniature electric screwdriver. In a second the face plate of the keypad was in his hand. Next, he brought out a small device that he had concocted, under Max's guidance, using spare parts from the Hellbat's repair kit. He affixed four wires to various points and pressed a switch. The security pad's display went haywire as Mike's makeshift scanner searched for the appropriate combination. This was followed by the telltale click of the door lock releasing. They were in.

"We have, at most, twenty minutes," Marcus informed him. "Perhaps less, if they have changed the guard schedules."

"Which is highly likely this week" Mike thought.

They entered through the hall door into what looked like a file storage room. Just inside the door, Marcus directed Mike to a smaller door off to one side that Mike might have otherwise taken for a janitor's closet. The back of the "closet" was a false wall. Behind that wall was the main computer room.

"There's another room just like this one down the hall," Marcus informed him, "…with much more ornate looking front doors of unbreakable glass. But the terminals in there are dummies. Try to use them and every alarm in the place goes off, and a metal grate falls across the entrance, trapping you inside. Even the security staff isn't supposed to know it's a fake, but in my previous life, I used to take one of the Emperor's secretaries to the bacchanals. She always talked too much when she was in her cups."

"Then it is a good thing that I've got you along, isn't it. But right now I need perfect silence." Mike commented.

Marcus nodded, but said nothing.

What came next, was actually not so difficult, at least not for Max. All computers, as far as Maureen and her systems team could surmise, would react to certain standard types of input according to their architecture and operating system. After a few test entries, Max would be able to analyze the response and extrapolate the system architecture. After that, it was just a matter of feeding in the new information using machine code, to eliminate the need for any high level languages. To let Max do this, Mike had to "empty himself" by using a kind of Zen exercise, that allowed Max to control his motor systems directly. Silence was also needed so that Max could listen through Mike's ears for the approaching guards on their rounds.

The first part of the operation went smoothly. Mike and Max had been practicing for the last two weeks. Marcus watched in amazement as, after a few hesitant tests, Mike's fingers took off, flying over the keyboard. It took just a little over twelve minutes to input and store all the information as well as to extract what he needed to know to create the appropriate passes.

Then, just as he was wrapping up, Max detected the approaching guard. From the sound, they were two corridors away. Max informed Marcus, without Mike even being aware. The young monk had already decided how he would handle it. Slipping out the door as silently as he could, he crept down the hall into the fake console room. Once there, he began pressing the keys on one of the keyboards, at random. Klaxons howled and the grate fell locking him in. Marcus didn't react. He continued pretending to be the desperate saboteur.

Almost immediately the alarm was silenced, and Marcus heard a key turn in the lock. The grate rose. As the door opened, he stood up, slowly, with his arms outstretched. Two young privates grabbed him roughly and spun him around to face the guard captain that had followed them in. There was a look of recognition in the captain's eye. In his former life Marcus had called him friend. No one spoke right off. Finally, just as the silence was becoming unbearable, it was broken by the guard captain.

"Well, if it isn't my old friend, Captain Marcus Ignatus," he said. There was still a small note of incredulity in his voice, mixed in with a large amount of sarcasm. "Your five years at the bottom of the river have been kind to you. Congratulations, I see that the gods of the underworld have promoted you, *Major*. Tell me, what brings you back to our side of the Stygian depths...eh?" Then to the privates, "Take him to guard post three and find out why he is here, how he got in, and which of the regional governors has suborned him.

"Do whatever you must and report back to me. But..," he added, "just the information, I don't want to know how you get it this time." Then turning to Marcus one more time he said, "I really am sorry, Old Friend – really I am."

"I believe you, Gaius, I really do, and I am sorry, too." Marcus told his former colleague and friend.

Captain Gaius Caligulus turned and left quickly. Watching him rush away like that, Marcus really did believe his apology. His old friend was a loyal servant of the Emperor, but he had never been able to accept the methods that his underlings were about to use in their attempt to extract information. The captain always left interrogations to his underlings, on the excuse that they needed the practice, and then he would feign great interest in the details to hide his "weakness". This time, however, he made it clear. He didn't want to hear a single word other than what was necessary.

As he heard the guard captain's heavy footfalls rushing down the corridor Marcus felt a great regret that things had turned out this way. *"If only we had a little more time,"* he thought, *"just a little more."*

The young privates, on the other hand, had none of their superior's problems. As they dragged Marcus from the room and down the corridor, their delight was obvious. They enjoyed their work! Guard post three was just two corridors away. At first glance, it looked like a normal office, no different from one you might find in any place of business. Until, that is, someone opened the cabinet that filled the better part of the longest wall. Inside were several racks of electrodes, all designed for different purposes, to attach to various parts of the victim's anatomy. Each was connected to one or the other of various power sources of increasing ranges of voltage and amperage. And, down in the corner, "just for old times' sake" a selection of irons, were kept red-hot in an electric brazier.

The pair of guards smiled maliciously at each other as they fastened Marcus to the chair and cut open his uniform front, being none too careful with the razor-like blade they used. There were a few rivulets of blood running down his chest as one of the young men turned back with a pair of electrodes in his hands.

"Now, I do hope you aren't going to be sensible, are you?" he asked, in a voice of sweet venom. "I mean that would take all the fun out of it, now, wouldn't it?" Marcus remained silent. He had already retreated far into the world of silence. He prayed, fervently, that this would buy Mike the time he needed to finish and get away.

Still at the console, Mike was oblivious to the first screams, even though they could be heard several corridors away. The guards had purposefully left the soundproof door open. The captain's office was well within earshot, too. These young whelps enjoyed tormenting more than just their immediate victim. Max had to keep it all from Mike until his job was complete or Marcus' sacrifice would be for nothing. As it was, Mike was instantly aware of Marcus' torture as soon as he came out of his "trance". Mike's first impulse was to get back to his men, if he was taken or if the chopper fell into government hands, all would be lost. But then there was another scream...

The way back to the chopper that Max had stored in his memory led right passed that room. Mike knew that he couldn't play the disinterested officer and just walk past while they abused his friend, especially since, as mission commander, he was responsible. Probably Max could dig another escape route out of information he took from the computer, if there was time. In all likelihood, Mike should be able to find another exit and get away from there undetected. There was just no possible way that he could ignore Marcus' cries.

Mike took a moment to compose himself, and then slipped out of the computer room, narrowly escaping detection by a replacement patrol. He feigned indifference as he passed by Guard Post Three. The new arrivals, just behind him, stopped to enjoy the 'spectacle' and joke with their confreres. Mike waited until they entered the office, readying himself mentally. He had never actually used these techniques outside of training before. He had decided that that was of no importance. With Max enhancing the necessary hormone systems and neurotransmitters he launched his attack. The replacement patrol went down before they had even cleared the office door. The first of the torturers, who was facing the door, charged Mike, trying to knock him off balance. Mike side stepped him easily. His blow to the guard's sixth vertebra put him out of action for a good while. His partner at the control panel, reacting to the ease with which Mike dispatched his comrades, panicked, attacking wildly. A roundhouse kick sent him flying backward, to land in the brazier of hot irons. He screamed in agony, ironically, everyone in earshot believed it was his victim screaming. Mike delivered one more blow, rendering him senseless. He pulled him off the brazier, and then turned to Marcus.

The monk was already bleeding from his nose and ears. Obviously, these clowns didn't care whether he told them anything or not. They were just amusing themselves. Mike cursed them under his breath as he unfastened his friend's bindings. He knew what Marcus' chances for survival were, but he couldn't bring himself to leave him among the 'heathens'.

Marcus was limp. His body was a dead weight, but thanks to Max's enhancements, it made little difference to Mike as he carried him, at a run, through the series of corridors and offices back to the chopper. He gave a remote signal that initiated the start-up sequence and charged on. He had his gun in his left hand. He wasn't worried about being discovered. If anyone challenged him, they wouldn't die by his hand, he had promised Ezra that, but in his anger at this barbarity, he was almost anxious to leave a few of them a permanent reminder of this night.

Mike regained the court yard without further incident. The occupants of guard post three were discovered at about the same time he reached the Hellbat. Gently he handed his load over to the others and climbed into the pilot's seat. He ordered Gabe to replace Marcus at the tactical station and launched the chopper. Although still running on stealth mode, Mike no longer hugged the roof tops. That took too much time. He pushed the craft to its limits, climbing and accelerating to Mach speed at the same time. Already, he could see the slow moving aircars rising in a futile bid to intercept him. At the last minute, just as the helicopter hit Mach three, Mike dropped the sonic barrier and adjusted his course to pass over the 'Pristine Palace'/White House. He was pretty sure that the Emperor would be making a rather late call for the imperial glazier that night.

Flying on full stealth mode once again, Mike turned for home. Already his mind was working overtime. It was possible that their discovery that night might cause the coming session to be postponed, or a check of the computer might find the information that Max had planted. The Security Forces could then sit back and wait for everyone to walk into a trap.

"Not to worry," Max informed him, *"the whole program is a worm, a Trojan Horse. No matter how carefully they check,*

nothing will show up. The information will not exist in the computer until the first validation is asked for, and then it will appear as though it had been there all along. As they have never had to worry about hackers planting worms in their systems, I doubt that they even know what to look for."

Mike breathed a little easier. Now, if he could convince the Security Force that he and his crew were destroyed, it would go a long way to assuaging this culture's natural paranoia. They just might relax again. He knew that he could count on a good deal of Patrician Conceit to help with the illusion. The troops that now pursued him were sure that they were more than a match for this "interloper".

"Radar indicates aircars rising from Castorus Base two kliks east, and another squadron rising from Brutus Barracks at New Caesarea, three kliks north-west," Gabe called.

It would have been simplest just to outrun them, but Mike had an idea.

Instead of accelerating away from the attackers, Mike began to decelerate.

"Scan for a large, unoccupied ground structure just outside of their weapons' range," he told Gabe. On his own console, he punched up an array of missiles.

"Got one," Gabe reported, "...two minutes away at present speed, heading three five zero degrees. Mike, it's the Arena."

"Perfect!" Mike thought.

He altered course. As he approached the designated area, his instruments confirmed what he expected would be the case. The intercepting squadrons were already firing upon them, hoping for a lucky shot. As he reached the stadium, Mike lurched and began to lose altitude. He shut down the sonic barrier again to give the impression that his systems were failing. He was sure that his pursuers had no idea what the proper sound of a fully functional Hellbat might be. He descended below the rim of the oval, and fired an assorted volley of incendiary and explosive warheads directly into the bowl of the Arena, followed by a full load of smoke bombs and tear gas. Then, at the last minute, under cover of the heavy smoke he veered off, with his stealth system reactivated.

On the scanners, Gabe could see the Security Force vehicles circling the inferno that Mike had just created. He relayed the information to Mike who acknowledged it without comment. Having eluded the Security Forces, he had only one thought. Although everything that he knew, and all his instincts, told him that there was no hope, Mike would not let go of Marcus so easily. If there was any chance at all, he would do whatever it takes... the thought was paramount as he altered course for home.

Hugging the ground again, Mike pushed the chopper for all she was worth. As soon as they were out of visual range, he began to accelerate and climb again, flying flat out for home. They arrived back in record time, but it was already too late. Mike wished that he had at least been able to do something back at the Ministry to ease the pain, but Moises assured him that Marcus hadn't lived long enough.

The rest of that night passed slowly for Mike. He refused Max's help to get to sleep, preferring to be awake and alone with his thoughts. He wondered if the General felt like this every time he lost someone under him.

At dawn, Jillian came to get him. There was a funeral for Marcus, and she knew that he would want to be there. The mass was simple and short, followed, as Mike expected, by a period of meditation in which everyone joined. Much of it surprised Mike. While most individuals were feeling sad at their loss, the ceremony spoke of hope and life. It was yet another new experience to ponder on, when he had the time. Right then, there were things to be done that would insure that his friend's death would not be in vain.

Back in New Rome/Washington, the night had not been a good one for the command of the Security Force either. They had combed the Ministry of Information Processing for any sign that the intruders had actually penetrated the real computer complex. Every inch of the real computer room had been dusted for finger prints, but none were found, Mike and Marcus had worn surgical gloves. The 'experts' had run all the system tests that they could think of, but found no sign of Max's worm. At the same time, others had examined, as closely as they could, the ruins of the Arena, which were still radiating a fierce heat. Finally, it was time to report to the Emperor.

His Imperial Highness was not in a good mood. He, too, had passed a miserable night. As it happened, last evening he had elected to spend a few pleasant hours with Calista, one of his favorite concubines. It had always been the case that whatever Calista had asked for he gave her, so long as her requests were not unreasonable. They never were. One such request, however, had been for a ceiling mirror above the bed. The idea actually tickled the Emperor and he granted the request. At the same time that Mike shattered all of the windows in the Imperial residence, they had been locked in passionate embrace. The imperial favorite had escaped injury when the mirror shattered because she was protected by the ample body of her lord. He was not so fortunate. Sitting, even on the softest chair, was quite painful.

The Minister of Imperial Security, and his Chief of Operations arrived to brief his Imperial Highness, just as the Emperor was 'motivating' a servant to greater zeal in fulfilling his latest request.

The poor man came scrambling through the door of the Oval Office followed closely by a flying paper weight that narrowly missed its target.

"When I say soft seat cushions, I mean SOFT seat cushions," the Emperor roared after him.

"My Lord," the Minister began, tentatively, from the door, bowing deeply as he spoke.

"Enter," the Emperor commanded. "Report!" he roared.

"Does your Imperial Highness wish all the details?" the Minister asked.

"Just the salient points," the Emperor said in a slightly more civilized tone.

The Minister signaled to the Chief, whom he had left standing at the door. He, too, bowed deeply as he entered the office.

"Exalted Highness," he began, "To begin, we can assure you that the attackers that caused your Glorious Lordship such trouble last night have most certainly been completely destroyed. Furthermore, my people have ascertained, beyond all doubt, that the vigilant guard staff at the Ministry of Information Processing intercepted the intruders before they could accomplish their sabotage."

"You are sure that sabotage was their intention? Who were they? Were you able to salvage anything of that strange craft for analysis?"

"We are certain, my Glorious Lord, that sabotage was indeed their intent, and that they were completely fooled by the decoy computer room – despite assistance from a treacherous deserter from our forces. The traitor was questioned, prior to his liberation, by his successor, but revealed nothing before he died. We have not been able to gain much useful information from the interrogators, however, they are still in shock, so brutal was the attack upon them. We can surmise that, apart from this Marcus Ignatus, they were untrained thugs. This is evidenced by the large number of assault troops used in the attack. The privates were able to tell us that they were set upon by a force of at least ten men."

"Further, from this, and from other reports that we have been following, we believe that the attackers were Christian Zealots. We have recently been checking into reports that an individual known only as 'Marek', a zealot known for the barbarity of his raids, was headed our way. Until now, we had no information about what he was planning. It is obvious that he thought that he could succeed with this wild sabotage scheme."

"And to answer your third question, we have not yet been able to get very near to the Arena, where they crashed. That is one reason why we can be sure that they all perished. The fire caused by their crash was so intense that many neighboring residences caught fire from the extreme heat. Nobody and nothing could have survived that inferno. Over flights reveal that the interior of the bowl was reduced to a puddle of molten steel, even the concrete melted."

The Emperor listened to the report, shifting his considerable weight around gingerly. Afterward, he asked one more question of the Minister.

"And the Imperial Session? Should we postpone it?" he asked.

"Not necessary, Divinity", the Minister answered with an authoritative air of assurance. "It is absolutely certain that we have eliminated this threat, and we will continue to meet any further attempts against your Imperial Majesty with equal efficiency."

"With greater efficiency," the Emperor responded, shifting himself again, as the servant returned with two enormous pillows. The Minister and his Chief of Operations simply bowed in response and, at a signal from their ruler, left the Oval Office as quickly as good grace would allow.

Straight from breakfast, Mike headed for his lab. Working in concert with Max, he set up the necessary programs to create the security badges for the Imperial Session. Work went slowly, Mike found that even with all Max's help, he couldn't concentrate on the task at hand. He was still working at noon when Anna came by, with a tray for two. She set it down on work table off to one side. Mike could see that she had been crying. He stored his current workspace and went to join her. Marcus' death had been especially hard on her. In the short time they had known each other, Marcus had become like a father to Anna. She needed to talk.

It was late afternoon when Anna finally left. Mike didn't regret the time spent with her either. He realized that there was a lot that he had to work out, too. Listening to Anna had helped him greatly. He returned to his work more focused, with a renewed determination. Again, he wondered if that was how the General might react, too.

As Mike was feeding the last of the security passes he had produced on the laser printer, into his make-shift laminator (a converted microscope slide sealer), Jillian brought another tray with his supper.

"You were missed at dinner," she told him. "Aaron wants me to remind you that we have a final briefing before bed tonight. Will the passes be ready?" she asked conversationally.

Mike showed her the ones that he had just finished.

"No difference between these and the real thing," he assured her. He rummaged in the box of passes for a second and pulled one out. "Here is yours," he said, "complete with the mandatory bad photograph."

Jillian examined the pass, wincing at the photo, but smiling approvingly at the quality of the production. Although no one could be one hundred percent certain that they would work, they seemed to have a 'feel' of authenticity. She told Mike that, and he thanked her. Max thanked her, too, but Mike didn't pass it on.

The room was alive with speculation when Jillian and Mike arrived for the final briefing. Rumors had been circulating about changes to the final plan. They greeted Mike with a barrage of simultaneous questions. In his usual style, he sat down and waited quietly, allowing them all to talk at once, until everyone realized that it was getting them nowhere.

As the last murmurs died away, Mike took the floor. His first word was simply, "Yes!" He then sat down again as the expected eruption of simultaneous questions exploded once more. When the room was again silent, Mike moved to the blackboard on which he had previously outlined their old strategy. Already the board contained a top down view of the capitol building, showing the many details supplied by Brother Marcus, and another building a short distance away, without details. It was identified as the New Rome Central Power Plant. Mike now erased the old drawing of the power plant and replaced it with one detailing the interior of the building. He also added an auxiliary structure to the Capital Building that he later explained was underground. Also, Mike added in another underground structure, or rather a series of structures, radiating from (and conversely, running to) many of the government buildings. All the while, the assembled strike teams watched in silence.

As soon as he finished, Mike returned to the table. He glanced around the room. There were questions on every face, but all held their tongues. Mike started by repeating the word "Yes."

"There are some very major changes," he announced, "and they may very well guarantee our victory. From our foray into the computer complex at the Ministry of Information Processing I have learned of the two key elements in the Emperor's personal security system. The first is that underground chamber attached to the Capital Building, the second is what, on the diagram, appears to be a network of tunnels, that is what it is."

"The room attached to the Capital Building is an auxiliary power facility. It is almost totally self-sufficient, requiring only periodic verification. It is overseen by a select crew, handpicked by the Emperor himself. Access is controlled by automated check points, and apart from the maintenance crew, this generating system is known to only a very few of the most trusted members of the Imperial Guard. The only way anyone gets in is if someone, very high up, makes an entry into the main computer, telling the security system to admit them. As such, anyone who passes the first stage of the system's security is able to continue without human challenge. This is because with such a pass their authority to be there is obviously without question. The importance of this facility is that it provides the power for all Imperial Security, including the power grid for the vehicles of Emperor's Personal Security

Force, and for that system of tunnels which I just drew."

"What the tunnel system is must seem obvious to you. It is an escape route. No one but the Emperor has access to it. The tunnels contain a series of power grids to power, what on my world we call a subway, a system of underground vehicles travelling on wheels like the bus we arrived in and the three others that arrived here. It appears that the use of the wheel as a mode of transport has not been totally forgotten. It may even be that, since the advent of the aircar, successive Emperors actually have suppressed such rudimentary technology in order to have a specialized getaway system for themselves. Whatever the case, if we shut down the auxiliary power station at the Capital Building, the Emperor will be unable to escape using the subway cars. Keeping that in mind, here are the augmentations to our original plan.

"To begin, we need to take out the main power station that powers the regular Security Force's aircars and communications. That one is easy enough to do. It is isolated by the security wall. A couple of missiles from the Hellbat and it will be just a pile of rubble. The bulk of forces in that sector will then be running on their emergency reserves. According to their specifications their power reserves will last for twenty minutes at most. As there is no fissionable or radioactive material present in the structure there should be no collateral damage."

"What about worker casualties?" Aaron asked.

"Hopefully none…" Mike answered. "If we approach and shoot from the south side of the structure we can take out the cold fusion unit safely without damage to the control sector on the north side. The only time there is anybody on the southern end of the building is during the maintenance cycle, which was just completed last week. There shouldn't be anybody in that area when we make our move."

He pointed to the underground power station next to the Capital Building. Taking out this station is critical. As I said, it powers the Emperor's escape system. If we shut down the power for his subway, there is no way that he can use the subway to make his getaway. He'll be stuck in the Capital Building. The one problem is that it isn't a cold fusion reactor. It is a controlled fission reactor. We used to have them on my world. This has to be done right.

To ensure that he cannot escape, we need to shut that reactor down and make sure that no one can restart it. According to the design specifications in the computer, it has a single emergency shutdown switch. Once that switch is tripped, the reactor shut-down can't be stopped. Once anyone shuts down the main control circuits, three other circuit paths, need to be reset before the start-up process will cycle. So, what we need to do is get a small team into the reactor room. Once the shutdown switch is tripped, they will have to disable the control console. Without the console, there is no way to restart the power, and the Emperor's emergency subway remains off line.

We will still also need to station people at the Emperor's emergency hatches. I've marked them here." Mike pointed out the locations of the Emperor's secret exits located around the senate chamber. There is always the possibility that he might try to hide in the tunnels, to give his security forces the chance to counter attack. Finding him could take more time than we would have. If his forces can actually mount a rescue attempt, civilians will get caught in the middle. That is how people get hurt, especially non-combatants. We don't want that. It is imperative that the Emperor is taken in the Senate Chamber, as quickly as possible.

For the next three hours Mike outlined the revised plan and made assignments, accepted or rejected suggested improvements, and rehearsed the various teams on the entire operation. By the time they broke up, everyone was clear on his or her role. Mike was just a little less nervous.

"They aren't real shock troops," he said to Max, *"but they are the best team that any commander could hope for in all other respects".*

"You're right on both counts; they have a lot of heart." Max answered. *"It doesn't seem to have stopped you from worrying though."*

"I can't help it, Max. They have become very important to me; particularly Jill, of course. We have only had eight weeks to train for this and now there are so many changes."

"Even experienced combat troops have losses, you know that, Mike."

"Lost in thought again?" Jill asked.

Mike jumped, as he often did when someone disturbed him during a chat with Max.

"Actually, I was chatting with a good friend," Mike told her. Then, seeing that they were alone in the briefing room, Mike gave in to an impulse, and he told her about his link with the living AI.

"And that's how I have been able to work things out with Gillian back home," he concluded.

"So you will be going home when tomorrow's done?" she asked, despondently. She already knew the answer. Mike only nodded. Even though she wasn't his Gillian, it was still so difficult to see her hurt. Then all of a sudden Jill seemed to brighten up.

"Look at me," she said, straightening herself up, mentally. "I am behaving like a spoiled child. I should be happy for you. Wanting only my way is not being very loving, is it; especially when you have already risked your life for us, and are preparing to do it again tomorrow." She stretched up and kissed Mike on the cheek. "Good night, '*Electric Company One*'," she said, using his code name, "We had all better get some sleep." Smiling at him one last time, Jillian turned and walked out of the room.

"Good night, Electric Company Two" he called after her. Keeping her on his team meant that he could know where she was during the operation, but the special nature of his mission also meant greater danger. He was still questioning his wisdom on that one.

"The more I experience this human emotion called love, the more it amazes me," Max told him.

"Me, too," was all Mike answered, as he collected up his notes.

"She will be in danger anywhere she is, Mike," Max said. *"You can only protect her so far. Maybe with us she has more of a chance."*

That, Mike realized, had been an unconscious part of his decision to keep her with him. With Max's help, maybe he could protect her from harm.

The next day started well before dawn. As always, it began with the community gathering for Morning Prayer. This day it was another combined service, both Jewish and Christians praying together. Just after the Christians in the group had received the Eucharist, Ezra rose in the solemn manner of a high priest. For half a moment Mike had visions of some prayer of the "smiting of our enemies" variety. That image was quickly dispelled by the effect that the holy man always had on him. To Mike, he was the embodiment of peace.

Ezra paused. The attention of the whole community was fixed upon him. Then in the traditional manner of his people, he lifted his hands in prayer. "Lord," he said, "for whatever will be, we give you thanks and praise, may your will be done in all things," and he sat down.

Nothing more was said. The community began their meditation; Mike, too, meditated with them. That he had adopted the discipline had ceased to surprise him. There were many things that Mike would be taking back to his own world when he returned; this would be one of them, if he survived the day.

The assault force for the capital was divided into three teams. As soon as breakfast finished the first contingent boarded the newly repainted Air Force buses. It was impossible to disguise its shape, but a little camouflage would get it to an access tunnel in the capital, over six hours away, much faster than any short range air car could. Mike said a "thank God" for the fuel depot that, along with the extra busses, had materialized just outside the weapons' storage. Without it, the bus would have quickly been useless.

A few days before, Mike risked bringing the original bus back to the service grill and then through the trees to the back entrance of the cave system for fueling. The teams boarded the bused at 06:00. Sam, who had become quite a proficient driver, drove the lead bus. He partially retraced the path that Mike had driven during their escape on the day of his arrival. Unlike that first day, he had to duck into the trees more than once to avoid the increased patrols that were assigned as added security for the opening of the Senate session. Just before the city he veered off towards New Rome.

Once at the outer wall of the capital, his passengers disembarked, and their group leaders led them into the service tunnels following Gabe's instructions. They had correctly reasoned that the access system was the same in New Rome as it was in New Caledon, where they had been enslaved. Each assault squad was made up of one hundred and forty men and women who had been in training intensively for the last seven and a half weeks. After accessing the service tunnels, they hid in an equipment depot. All slave work crews would be on lockdown for the first few days of the session, until the Security Squad could be sure that all of their positions were secure. Less stringent precautions had cost them in the past. The resistance teams now took advantage of that. It was always possible that Security might check their hiding place, but highly unlikely. They were positive that no one knew how to access the tunnels.

Once the last group had joined them, the full assault force moved out. They no longer worried about the patrols, as anyone they happened upon, or that happened upon them, they took captive. Making their way through the service tunnel, they came to the exit just across from the Cassius Barracks.

Meanwhile, Mike and his crew were busy loading equipment onto the Hellbat. The explosive grenades they were carrying in their "lunch boxes" needed to be sealed against any possible detection equipment, as well as visual inspection. The charges were hidden in pots of stew and stowed away in the lunch boxes; messy, but concealing.

"Why not just blow it up from the air?" someone had asked Mike the night before. No one in this continuum had ever seen a fission explosion, not even on film. There had never been one, at least not that the powers-that-be would let the people know about. "Besides," Mike added, "it is buried inside twenty-five feet of concrete and steel. They wanted to be sure that it if it ever went up the whole city wouldn't go with it."

"No, we have to shut it down first, and then completely disable the restart circuits. In a worst case scenario, we will destroy those circuits by force, but only if the fusion reactors are already off-line."

When the buses carrying the phony delegates and security forces was within range of New Rome, Mike took to the air. Again, Gabe was flying 'second seat'. Mike had discovered that he was a natural. After only eight weeks, Mike was confident that Gabe could manage the craft. He wouldn't stand up to an experienced combat pilot from back home, but with the Hellbat's systems to back him up he, and with Moises at tactical, could handle anything that the Imperial Forces could throw at them. At least that is what Mike hoped. It was their job to keep reinforcements out of the capital until the Emperor capitulated. After that, the fugitives would be the legitimate government according to the ways of this ancient system.

As before, he approached at tree top level on full stealth mode. This time, he had to approach on a parabolic course, coming in over the suburbs so as not to be spotted too early. Just out of sight of the power plant, the Hellbat touched down long enough for Mike and his team to disembark, and then Gabe retraced their flight path back to the edge of the city. He then altered course and climbed into the sun. According to the revised plans, Gabe was to hold position at fifty thousand feet, with the sun at his back, and wait for the Imperial Troops stationed at Brutus Barracks to react to any alarm that they might receive. His orders then were to blow the power station.

Their air cars had emergency power packs that would get them to the capital, if Gabe let them. Fortunately Mike, himself, had thought to scan them during their pursuit the previous night. The Hellbat's system now had an imprint of their engine's operating frequencies as well as that of their power packs. There was no way to jam all the aircars at once, but Gabe could still keep them from going anywhere if he rotated through the fleet, jamming and then releasing as many as he could each time. If all went well, Moises might never have to fire a shot.

Meanwhile, at Cassius Barracks, a contingent of the main assault group gained access to the station using their counterfeit identity badges, and wearing the uniforms taken from the captured patrols. What came next was the most dangerous part of this phase of the operation. Not only did they need to fool the men at the Barracks' main guard station, they needed to secure the command post before the next scheduled check-in. If the capital's main command post didn't receive an all-clear from the patrol units that were now being held by Sam's forces, a general alarm would be raised.

Each member of the primary assault team passed his ID over the scanner. After the system accepted their ID's the guard at the desk released the door lock. The three men at the desk greeted them with weapons at the ready.

"Who are you, then?" the desk sergeant demanded gruffly. "And why aren't you out on patrol."

Sam was ready with his answer: "We were just sent over from Brutus Barracks to act as back-up to your troops, under your commander, of course. Our orders are to report to him immediately upon arrival." He took a document from his breast pocket and presented it to the sergeant, who scanned it quickly and returned it to him. Mike's forgery worked like a charm.

"All right," the sergeant said, "go on through; the second door on the sinister. Leave your pulse rifles in that rack." He indicated a weapons rack next to the door. Sam nodded in salute, and proceeded to the indicated door, stowing their appropriated rifles as they went. Just as he was about to pass through the door the desk sergeant called, "Wait a minute!"

Sam and his group froze, not knowing what had gone wrong. Shlomo slipped his hand into his trouser pocket, feeling the butt of the twelve millimeter pistol concealed there.

"Your man's shoes there…" the sergeant said indicating Shlomo's footwear, "they aren't regulation."

"Good eye!" Sam countered. "He just transferred in from the regular forces for the week. We had to find him a hand-me-down uniform, but we had no shoes to fit those huge feet of his." At least that had been a half-truth. None of the patrol officers they captured had feet big enough to match Shlomo's shoe size.

"Well, see the Quartermaster after you're finished with the commander. We can't have him going around like that with all the big wigs in town. He probably has a better fitting uniform for him, too. This isn't the time to be poorly dressed!" He pressed the door release and the squad entered the corridor. Sam nodded again.

As the door closed behind them Shlomo was about to breathe a sigh of relief when Jesse whispered in his ear, "We're probably being watched; stay in character."

They continued down the hall to the second door on the left as instructed. Sam knocked and was admitted by the barracks' commander, who had most likely been given a heads-up by the desk sergeant.

"Men…" he began, but that was as far as he got. All six of members Sam's team drew pistols from their pockets. In short order, they disarmed the commander and his guards. Sam pressed the door override button on the commander's desk, releasing the front door lock. The rest of the assault squad rushed in with weapons at the ready. The men at the desk gave up without a fight. They had no idea what those strange weapons could do, and had no desire to find out.

With Sam and his team in the commander's office, they had full access to all areas of the barracks. It took very little time to corral everyone at the station. All prisoners were secured in the basement holding cells. The cells were packed so tightly that there was almost no room to sit down on the floor. The soldiers were stripped of their uniforms. The insurgents began by acquiring as many new uniforms as were available from the quartermaster's stores. If any more were needed they were taken from the best of the uniforms confiscated from the prisoners. Once everyone was outfitted in the best looking uniforms they could find, the Cassius Barracks insignias were removed and replaced with the Special Security Detail insignias Mike had created. Leaving a small contingent of people to guard the prisoners and maintain routine communications and check-ins, the majority of the assault force manned the Barracks' fleet of aircars and headed off toward the Senate Building.

Back on the ground, Mike and his team of three, including Jill, entered the power station. Their false passes worked like a charm. They entered the main station without anyone questioning their authority. Although they did attract a few glances as they descended directly to the lower level. At a second security access point their cards were accepted by the automated security system without question, but the Senior Operations Officer, wearing a uniform that looked more military than technical came chasing after them.

"Excuse me, Citizen Technicians," he called, "a moment, please." Although his manner was casual enough, Mike detected an undercurrent of discomfort in his voice. The four paused. The man approached puffing a little, and trying not to show it.

While it was most likely a Security Forces "plant" among the workers on the main desk who called the Senior-Op, out of curiosity. Still, for an instant Mike's heart sank. Had he missed something? Was there a secondary scan that had triggered an alert when it read their bogus badges? He had no idea when an internal signal might have activated when they entered. Their passes he created gave them enough clearance to get through every door. For anyone at the station, including the Senior-Op, their badges should have been authorization enough. But what if someone higher up was alerted; someone with the authority to ask questions?

"Relax," Max told him, *"I have reviewed the wiring diagrams. No such system exists, unless it is not in the computer. Considering the accuracy of the security details we have seen so far, there is no evidence to logically support such a supposition. Your assumption concerning human curiosity is the most likely answer."*

"I hope so, Pal. Or it's all in the dumper."

To the Senior-Op Mike gave his most engaging smile. "How can we assist you, Director?" he asked, sounding as polite as possible.

"It is customary, Citizen Technician, to check in with the Senior-Op, that's me, prior to proceeding down below. I know that it is not in the regulations, Citizen, but it is a courtesy."

Mike had noticed how the Senior-Op kept emphasizing the word "citizen" and now the word "courtesy". Then he remembered something in one of the briefings that Jill had given him. Just as in the Roman Empire of his world, originally only those born in Rome, or now New Rome, were citizens, "Patricians". But as the empire grew citizenship could be earned, but such citizens were second class. In stature they were still subservient to the Patrician class. This man was some sort of neo-Patrician whose nose was put out of joint because these "citizens" had not shown the proper respect for "one of his class". Mike had to be careful. He had to mix the right amount of ego-stroking with a strong reminder of their supposed special status. Even the Senior-Op could not go where they were going except in an emergency. (This was probably how the real technicians had gained their citizenship.) But he mustn't antagonize him enough that he would run a secondary check on them. He might try to hang on to them, just to show 'these provincials' that he had power, too. Just as he was about to answer the man with what he thought was a well-measured response, Jillian stepped in.

"Our apologies, Director," copying Mike, she used a title that was actually superior to the one he held, "but we have special orders. They come directly from the Imperial Office, from the Imperial Commander-in-Chief, himself. He wished to make sure that the earth tremor that destroyed the arena the other night has not damaged Sector Q. The Emperor was not satisfied with the Senior Inspection Officer's report. He is due to open the Imperial Session any minute. Are we to report back to the Emperor's Chief-of-Staff that you delayed us with customs and formalities at such a time, Senior Op?"

'Nice touch!', Mike thought. 'Start with a flattering title and finish with his real title, suggest exactly what he stands to lose.'

"But Mike, we destroyed the arena, there was no earth tremor."

"Check your files on propaganda. There was no way that the Imperium could admit that something like us could exist. They had to create an excuse."

The Senior-Op squirmed a bit, and then, obviously worried and embarrassed said, "Forgive me Citizen Technicians, (with deference this time), I should have realized that at this time only a vital task would have brought anyone down to Sector Q. Please excuse me. I will let you get back to your work."

As the Senior-Op hurried off, with a little less dignity than he normally demonstrated, the four breathed a collective sigh of relief.

"Good move, Jill!" Mike said. "Well done."

"But won't he check our story?" one of the others asked.

"He wouldn't dare," Jillian explained, "He has far too little authority to call the Pristine Palace himself, and he wouldn't risk calling his superiors. Our story made too much sense. He would be in as much, if not more, trouble if he blew the whistle and was found to be wrong. This way, he can defend himself with the high plausibility of our story."

Above, the assault teams arrived just as the delegates were entering the Senate building. The insurgents arrived, flying in in formation. As the aircars touched down they were immediately surrounded by Security Forces. When they recognized the insignia on the team's uniforms, the majority of them returned to their posts. The Senior Centurion remained along with a small contingent of men. He approached Adam who was dressed in a Legatus Legionis uniform and insignia.

"Welcome, Legate…" he began with deference. Adam paused. The Centurion continued, "I apologize for our initial reaction, but we were not informed in advance of your arrival, and these vehicles are not authorized."

Adam looked directly into the Centurion's eyes. The man immediately lowered his gaze with a look of abasement on his face, "Apologies." Inwardly, Adam smiled. He wasn't sure that he could pull it off, until he actually did it.

"Your vigilance is to be commended, Centurion," He told the man. "I will convey your efficiency to his Imperial Highness, when I see him later," he said, with just the right balance of disdain and praise. The Centurion nodded respectfully, careful not to speak unless he was directly questioned.

Adam handed him an envelope. "We were tasked by our divine Emperor to pick up these special delegates to the Imperial Council. As you can see, we were forced to commandeer alternative transport when our official motorcade was sabotaged by one of the provincial factions. Have as many of your people as you can spare ready to assist me. As soon as I have delivered these delegates and their aides…" he indicated the members of the team, who were dressed in very fashionable businesslike garb. (Each of the aids were carrying large cases, which actually contained assault rifles and other assorted weapons.) "…I intend to go to the Imperial Motor Pool and personally discover who has been co-opted."

"By your command!" the Centurion responded smartly. "If your delegates are ready, Legate, we will escort you and them into the Imperial section." He saluted smartly. Then he and his cohort took up positions around Adam and his team, and escorted them into the building.

Mike's team continued on to the access elevator to Sector Q. Each in turn placed their ID in the slot while they all held their breath. Mike knew the process that was now going on. At the Ministry of Information Processing, the main computer was cross-checking with more than a dozen independent databases. If Mike had missed even one of them, a security containment wall would fall trapping them, and then release a gas that would immobilize them until the Security Force could arrive.

With all the other security checks that were going on at the Capitol, the load on the Ministry system was extreme. It seemed to take forever. Then, finally, the elevator door opened. The ride to the lower level took only a few moments, but that, too, seemed to go on forever. It felt like they were descending into the bowels of the earth, not just three floors down.

A glance at his watch told Mike that he had little time to get everything done before the signal came in from their team that by now would be in the Imperial Ante-room, signalling the Emperor's arrival.

As soon as the elevator door on the lower level closed behind them Mike broke into a run, with the other three hard on his heels.

"We are behind. We have three minutes before the Emperor's scheduled arrival time," he reminded them. "He may be late, but we can't count on it. We have to disable the system as quickly as possible. Peter, get to work on the security system. That's got to be shut down first. We don't want to alert anyone to our activities."

"And we don't want that confinement wall falling down on us either," Peter answered. "I don't feel like a nap just now."

That was a sentiment with which Mike was in full agreement, as he and the others set to work removing the cover plates from control panels. There was a lot that they could get done while Peter did his work. The one weak point, Mike conceded, was that disabling the security system would unlock the door to Sector Q. If anyone noticed, station security would be down there in a split second, and it then might all be over. The lights on the security console went green. Peter triggered the shut down cycle. The reactor began to cycle down.

Above them, the Centurion led Adam and his contingent directly into the ante-room of Emperor's private offices. On arrival, he turned to Adam. "When you are ready, Legate, as many of my troops as I can spare are at your disposal." He saluted smartly and departed, followed by his men. As the door closed behind them, the "aides" opened their cases. Everyone set to the task of re-assembling the weapons the cases contained. They moved quickly. There was no way of knowing whether the Emperor would be early, late or on time. They had just enough time to assemble their weapons, when the signal sounded to announce the Emperor's arrival.

"Places everyone…" Adam instructed. The group fanned out. Many of those in security uniforms took up key positions in the main hall. They all wore adequate rank insignia to move about without challenge by regular forces. One or two still had to do some fast talking when their strange weapons were challenged, but a little bluster and feigned superiority were sufficient to get them through. In the imperial ante-room the "delegates" simply sat in the chairs around the room looking busy, their guns carefully concealed. Adam and three of his Centurions stood in guard positions.

Adam signalled Mike in the reactor room below, as he heard the entourage approach. The first people to enter were the members of the advance security sweep. The lead Centurion was surprised to see a Legatus Legionis present, as his own commander was walking with the Emperor. He was about to call out when Molly produced her M-35 and pressed it to his head. In his position he had been briefed about the incident with the man in the arena with the strange weapon. It seemed that loyalty until death was not what it used to be. Adam relieved him of his communicator, and called in the all clear code. Moments later, when the Emperor entered, the entire team that had stayed behind in the anti-room emerged from their various places of concealment.

Below them, Mike's concern over the alarm was almost a self-fulfilling prophecy, when the Senior-Op, with five armed guards, casually walked in. It seemed that he had not been sufficiently cowed after all, and had decided to run a status check on the station, hoping to trip them up in their work. Only he had found more than he had expected. Peter had just finished sabotaging the alarms when the report of it came up on the Senior-Op's board. He wasted no time trying to ring disabled klaxons. Instead, he grabbed the nearest guards at hand, and made tracks for Section Q with weapons at the ready.

Now he stood there grinning smugly. "So, citizens..." This time the word was truly used as an insult. "I don't know which faction in the Assembly of Governors has co-opted you, but you are about to find out that the risk was definitely not worth it. The Empire generously lavished money on your training, and even gave you, provincials – another insult – 'citizenship'."

Just then the receiver on Mike's belt beeped once, only he and Jillian heard it. The Emperor had arrived upstairs. The Senior-Op was so absorbed in his gloating that he missed the subtle signal. As he continued with his diatribe Mike and Jill knew that they had to act, right now!

The Senior-Op continued, "You can be assured that your punishment will be measured out with the same measure as the gracious gifts that you have received. Indeed, the Emperor, himself, will probably elect to personally decide your fate. Be sure that he will not take your treacherous ingratitude at all lightly."

It was obvious that the Senior-Op was really enjoying his revenge. The security officers were also revelling in the images that he attempted to conjure, so much so that they relaxed their vigilance ever so slightly. They missed it when Jillian leaned back on the console to verify that the shutdown protocol was complete. The guards took Mike's standing with his head bowed as a sign of abject failure. They couldn't know that Mike was marshalling all his resources as well as calling on Max to kick all of his systems into an endocrine overdrive.

"All the way, Partner," he told him. Max complied.

In the ante-room above, Adam addressed the Emperor, "Emperor Hannibal XIV, we are the 'Revolution of Hope'. We do not wish to do you any violence, but we have deemed it necessary to offer you the choice. We can either escort you into the Senate Chamber, where you will publically surrender to us, or we will carry your lifeless body to be displayed to all the delegates. We would prefer the former. For we are sure that either way, once they are in the custody of our people, already positioned in the chamber, the Governors assembled here will swear their loyalty to us.

At that moment the Emperor's Legate proved that loyalty till death was not totally gone from the empire, as he attempted to shield the Emperor with his body while drawing his sidearm. Three others in the retinue did the same. All fell to the superior firepower of Adam's team. It was the Emperor who now stood with his head bowed. "We surrender. Take us to the Senate Chamber," he said in a subdued voice.

"Adam pressed the muzzle of his 12mm pistol into the small of the Emperor's back. "Two warnings your highness: we have men and women throughout the hall disguised as security forces, and you have just seen what our guns can do; if you try to summon help, no one will be able to come to your aid. The second, I think is obvious…" he pressed the pistol a little harder into the he Emperor's back. As one, they moved into the Emperor's box.

When Mike raised his head to face the Senior-Op, he launched into action. It seemed to the guards that he was flying. Three fell without even seeing him. He took the fourth and fifth with ease. Only the Senior-Op got off a shot, striking Jill squarely in the chest. The force of his blast threw her over the emergency console. At the same instant Mike hit him. The full force of his amplified abilities was magnified by his fury. In spite of his helmet, the back of the Senior-Op's skull was splintered by the blow. Its force hurled him forward virtually shattering his facial plate, and demolishing his features beyond recognition. Peter and Timon were stunned by the speed and ferocity of Mike's assault. He grabbed the pair and thrust them through the door of the control room, slamming it behind them.

With no other alternative left to him, Mike fell back on his plan of last resort. He dumped the pot of stew from his lunch box, and ripped grenade out of its protective bag. He pushed it into the heart of the main control console, and pressed the button that activated a three second countdown. Nothing could stop it.

Mike launched himself over the control console. If there was any chance that Jillian was still alive he had to make sure that she was as protected as she could be from the blast. As he cleared the top of the console, he had just enough time to see her, crumpled up on the floor, before he heard the whine in his ears. Mike never landed behind the security console, never felt the explosion that demolished the reactor controls. He landed on the shift pad in the *Project Symphony* control room.

He had only a brief moment to consider what might have happened to Jillian.

"Max," he called.

"Sorry, Mike," came the AI's reply. *"The General ordered me to pull you out, and I had no grounds on which to argue with him."*

That was all that Max had time to say before the after-effects of his massive augmentation of Mike's systems kicked in, throwing Mike into convulsions. Just before passing out, Mike looked up to see a very worried Gillian rushing into the shift chamber.

Medics took Mike to the makeshift base hospital where Dr. Gauthier pumped him full of sedatives. He also gave Max orders to shut down certain systems while fortifying others. Max responded that he had been awaiting those orders, and was beginning immediately. For the next several hours Mike slept, though his sleep was anything but peaceful.

Seeing Jill lying on the reactor control room floor, an instant before shifting, and then an instant later seeing Gillian in the shift chamber, played havoc with Mike's subconscious mind. He kept having nightmares in which Jill and Gillian were being continually interchanged. In one dream, it was Gillian who was in the reactor control room and Jill who waited for him back home, while in another, Jillian was blown to bits to be reassembled as Gillian who was then shot by a faceless Senior-Op. All the while, Max could only observe and record the neural data. There was no way anyone could help Mike.

Finally, Mike awoke. His movement roused Gillian, dozing in a chair at his bedside. Mike reached out and pulled her to him and held her tightly. It was a long time. When he released her, Mike slid over in the bed. Without a word, she lay down beside him and enfolded him in her arms. She softly stroked his hair, as he slipped off into a gentler sleep.

It was three days before Dr. Gauthier agreed to release Mike from the hospital. He arrived home to find Gillian waiting.

"Max gave me your access code," she told him.

"You're a great wife, giving me away so soon?" Mike asked.

"You were already spoken for when we said 'I do'. I'm just recognizing the prior claim. Besides, I prefer to be thought of as your 'alter-ego' not your spouse."

Mike winced, *"Fair enough"* he said, and then had to explain his reaction to Gillian.

"Oh, yes, I know. Max and I had a long talk about that. You know, he really does sound like another you. Even his humor is the same as yours. You 'guys' must get along really great."

"We're doing alright. But how would you feel about living with two guys at the same time? I can promise you that my alter-ego is very discrete."

"Yes, we all know. The General had a hairy fit the first time Max refused to report what was going on."

"When was that, Max?"

"Your first night, with Jillian"

"Yes, I see."

"Well?" Gillian asked.

Mike told her the story. It didn't surprise him when Gillian was not disturbed by it. Instead, she simply said, "Poor girl, she must have been devastated. I would have been, in her place."

"She was strong, Jill was." Mike fell silent. Then, after a time, he turned to Gillian. "I am going to go back. I have to, you know. I have to find out what happened. If they lost, I have to destroy that munitions dump and, I can't issue a remote destruct for the Hellbat from our continuum. – And, I need to know..."

"...what happened to her, to Jillian." she finished.

"Yes," Mike said quietly, "Besides you, she was the first woman who was not a colleague, that I could call a friend since I was a kid. I have to know."

"Yes, you do," was all the Gillian said. After that, they just sat there in silence.

As they were finishing supper, General Urnbreach arrived with Maureen. Gillian had invited them for dessert and coffee. Instinctively, Gillian maneuvered Maureen out into the kitchen while Mike told the General what he wanted to do. The General listened quietly, and then, for a long moment, considered the various arguments Mike had presented.

"If you must, then I'll support you," he said, and then raising his voice he bellowed, "You girls can come in now. We're done." and turning to Mike he said "Reminds me of my childhood. Whenever we had guests, my mother used to take the wives into the kitchen 'so the men could talk'". She was very old fashioned. As Maureen volunteered to pour the coffee, he said, "Just a small one, Love, we have an early morning tomorrow, someone," he feigned annoyance as he indicated Mike, "wants to go back," adding, "you have to admire a man who doesn't like leaving things unfinished."

The next morning, there were very few surprised

comments. Only a few people, who didn't know Mike all that well, expressed any shock. Shift time was set for 09:00, as Mike walked in, Urnbreach handed him the remote that would destroy the Hellbat, if necessary.

"It has been augmented," he told Mike. "We lost five attack helicopters and a number of planes. If there are any more there, that your friends don't know about, and the old regime is still in power, this will send out a general destruct order. And if the takeover was a success..." he flipped a switch. "...This will locate any other bird in that continuum. If you need them, there are short instructions on the back."

"Understood, Sir, and thank you."

"Seeing as all our hardware and real estate doesn't seem to want to come back with you, we want to make sure that the nastier stuff doesn't end up in aggressive hands."

"I don't mean this..." Mike said, indicating the remote. "...I mean for letting me go back."

"I know. It's something you just have to do, I respect that. Good luck, son."

As he stepped into the shift chamber, he threw the older man a casual salute. The General nodded, with a slight smile.

"*He's still nervous,*" Max commented, adding, "*Oh, and we're going back to the cavern hideout.*"

Mike had just enough time to acknowledge him, before the wave that he knew to be the shift effect hit him, and when it subsided, he was in the main entry cavern of the fugitive's hideout. All around him were crates of supplies and equipment. There was a great deal of activity, but it was all in the surrounding rooms, evidenced only by the sounds that echoed back to him. Mike suddenly realized that he had no way of knowing who was in control here. Then a voice from behind caused him to freeze.

"You there, among the crates, don't move."

For half a moment Mike was stone still, and then he recognized the voice, just as the speaker recognized him.

"Colonel Mike, is that you?" Gabe asked, incredulously. "Thank heaven, it is you!"

As Mike turned to face his friend, the young man placed his weapon on a nearby crate and swept Mike up in a bear hug, nearly crushing him.

"We all thought that you had been blown up in the power station. Peter said that you pushed him and Timon out the door, and then the whole room exploded. They were then taken by the guards, But by then the Emperor had fficially surrendered to Adam. It meant that they were in custody for about three minutes. Once it was official, we had the control of the Capital Building and Sam ordered the staff to get the door to the Sector Q control room open. Only when they did, all they found was Jillian, unconscious, on the floor behind the security panel. – Jill!" Gabe exclaimed, cutting himself off, mid-sentence, "Here I am blathering along like an idiot and saying nothing. You are just the person that she would want to see. She has been hardly eating or sleeping, the physicians are worried about her recovery. You could…"

Mike grabbed Gabe, "Jillian is alive? I saw her shot."

"Yeah, I know," Gabe answered matter-of-factly, "but the station guards have only stun blasters. Can't have the big military ones going off in a place like that. One wrong shot and..," he finished his sentence by motioning in the air like a great explosion.

For a moment Mike was ready to burst, when Gabe didn't continue. The young man burst into a grin.

"She's in the infirmary. I think you know where that is?" he asked, still imitating the Cheshire cat (although he had never heard of it).

His wry humor was lost on Mike just then. He pushed the locator/destruct unit into Gabe's hands.

"Here – instructions are on the back–just don't press the wrong button," he called over his shoulder as he was already threading his way through the crates towards the tunnel to the back entrance.

He found Jillian dozing, fitfully. Her left arm had been injured and was in a plastic cast unit. Its indicator color showed that the break had been treated with a bone knitter and would be healed in another couple of days. Whether she broke it, when the stunner sent her flying over the console, or during the blast, Mike couldn't tell.

"And you'll never know unless you ask her," Max commented, adding, *"From the look of it, waking her up might*

be a favor."

Mike had to agree. He knew why he was stalling. This would probably be the last time they would see each other. Mike wasn't prepared for this. Jillian had been, until now, an as yet, unhealed wound of this adventure. She stirred fitfully, and Mike stroked her hair. Jill woke at his touch. Mike could see from her expression, that she was confused, unable to be sure that she was awake. He stroked her hair again and she smiled, softly.

"I can't move," she said, sleepily. Then, as Mike opened his mouth to speak she explained, "I mean that I dare not. I'm still not sure that it's really you. If this is just dream, then moving might wake me up, and I want it to last just a little while longer."

"It's no dream," Mike assured her. "Though I suppose that if it was your dream, I would probably say that."

"You probably would," Jill agreed, and she reached out and touched his hand. "We thought that you were dead, or worse, that you had somehow been taken by one of the segments of the guard, before the Emperor surrendered. Few people ever survive their interrogation techniques. I would sooner have found your body in the rubble."

"No, Max pulled me out before the explosives went off. It's ironic. I thought that you were dead. If I had known that you were still alive, I might have delayed long enough to get you out of the room."

"And we would have lost," Jill told him, flatly. "You

did the right thing." Aaron told me that some kind of alarm had been raised when we shorted out the security system. The Emperor might have tried to rabbit. If he had, we would never have gotten another chance."

"I suppose that now you and your people will return to the city, and take up the reins of power?" Mike asked.

"Some, my father and the council are still in the Capital, which they are thinking of renaming in your honour. Fr. Lawrence and members of the Peter & Paul Community, along with Ahmet and Ishmael have joined him. They and the other resistance groups are busy consolidating their hold on the new government. They have to be very careful not to throw the baby out with the bath water, as they set up the new system. Corrupt, paranoid and despotic as it may have been, the imperial hierarchy still contained the mechanisms for implementing the structures of the ancient republic.

As for the rest of us, many are going to remain here. We have a hospital to run, remember. Supplies are being shipped in to convert our oversized hidey hole into a real living space. You have given us a purpose with your hospital here, and you would be pleasantly surprised to know how far our physicians and – what did you call them, *nurses*? – have gotten in your CATS program." As evidence, she held up her treated arm. "We are learning, fast. In fact, once the community health centre is up and running, I am going to get back to my training. I want to be a doctor, too."

"You are not so different from the Gillian of my continuum," he told her.

At the mention of Gillian, Jill became very quiet. "I don't suppose that you came back here because she gave you your walking papers?" she asked, her voice barely a whisper.

"No," Mike answered, as quietly, "I didn't even know that you were still alive. I came back, because I had to know."

"Had to know?"

"Whether it was a success; maybe to destroy the weapons cache if necessary. And..," Mike faltered.

"And?" Jillian asked, almost daring to hope.

"And to find out..., you know. I had to know what happened to you; if necessary, to see your dad once more."

Mike could see that it was not the answer that Jillian had hoped for.

"Jill, you are special!" he told her, trying to sound as earnest as possible. "I am only sorry that I..," again he faltered.

"No, you're not," Jill told him quietly, through a sad smile. "You're sorry that you have to hurt me. Mike, you're a far better person than you give yourself credit for, and Gillian is one very lucky girl for having you."

Before Mike could respond, she reached out with her good arm and pulled him close, kissing him with all the passion that she felt. Mike didn't resist. He was emotionally torn, but he couldn't deny her. In this embrace, he felt all that was missing from her first kiss that very long eight weeks ago.

After a moment she released him. "Good-bye, my love." she whispered.

As if given leave to go, Mike stepped back from the bed.

"Do it," he thought, and the hospital room faded into the shift chamber, where Gillian was waiting.

Only, Gillian was not waiting alone. Somehow, Reall had learned of this second trip, and had returned in hopes of catching the General in an unauthorized operation. He had brought several of the base's security officers along. It was obvious that he was intending to take control, and place the General under arrest.

As the whine in his ears subsided, Mike heard him attempting to do just that. "By the authority given me by the United States Senate and confirmed by the Penatgon," (General Urnbreach could guess which Generals), "I am taking comm–" He never finished his statement.

The sound of those few words was all that Mike needed to hear. His eyes immediately went to Reall's left hand. He closed the distance between them and flattened the Senator with a single blow; without any help from Max. Reall lay stunned on the floor of the Console room. As the guards began to advance, Mike drew his pistol, released the safety and aimed it directly at the Senator's head. The guards retreated.

"Mike, son, I don't know what you're thinking, but this won't help me any..." the General began.

Mike cut him off. "This isn't about helping you, sir." He turned back to Reall. The fury in his voice was unmistakable. "Finally, I can put a face to the voice and the hand that is forever seared into my memory.

"Senator Jansen Reall, I am placing you under arrest for the cold-blooded murder of Dr. Michael Kelly, my father, and it would be a great favour to me if you would please try to escape." He looked Reall in the eye as he spat out each word.

The Senator looked back, stunned by the turn of events. At first he cringed in terror on the floor. Then he tried bravado, but his voice trembled when he spoke. "Those are baseless lies. You have no proof!"

Without warning the gigantic master monitor in the control room changed. The image showed the console in the treehouse those many years ago, as seen through Mike's eyes. Almost everyone realized that Max was channelling Mike's memory of that fateful moment.

First, Max played the earlier memory of the lead man-in-black brutalizing Mike's father. Reall's voice was clear and crisp as it played through every speaker in the room. The image of his left hand with the unique yin/yang tattoo was two feet high on the gigantic screen and crystal clear. Next, came the scene following the SCORCH, as he raised his gun and shot Mike senior. As the shot echoed through the Shift Chamber, Mike advanced on Reall.

The ferocity in Mike's face told the story of the anger that consumed him at that moment. His weapon was trained on Reall. No one else in the room moved a muscle. Even the guards stepped further back. Mike looked Reall in the eye: "Go on, RUN!" he yelled. "RUN!"

The senator peed his pants and started to cry. "Pleassssse, pleeeeeassse don't kill me." He whimpered.

Mike lowered his gun. Turning to the guards he quietly said. "Please take out the trash. The charge, as previously mentioned, is capital murder…"

The General stepped up, "…and High Treason!" he added. Under his breath he added, "That bastard's gonna swing, by God I swear it!"

He put his hand on Mike's shoulder and looked him in the eye, "Your father would be very proud of you today, Colonel – son – I know I am. If it'd been me, I would have shot him dead."

"I'm proud of you, too, Michael." Rob Gauthier told him.

Gillian threw her arms around his neck and kissed him. For a very long moment, he just held her close.

Epilogue

Senator Reall's trial was held in-camera, as was permitted by the charge of High Treason. Files from his "other office" in Washington had proven to be quite illuminating. They showed that Reall, and his cohort of renegade black-ops agents, had sold out to the cartels. The drug lords wanted the shield technology, badly. With it they would have been invincible. Just the fact that Reall was attempting to force Mike senior into giving them access to that technology was adequate proof of their crimes. Initially, the disgraced senator was sentenced to hang. Technically, that was still the penalty for treason, even in the late 21st Century. He would have been hanged, too, if Mike had not petitioned the President to commute his sentence to life-without-parole.

"I'm sure that it's what my dad would have wanted. It was why he worked on systems that were meant to keep people alive. He let others design the 'machines of death', as he called them," Mike explained, when the General asked. "Besides, I also arranged for him to be sent to a super-max prison. This 'man-of-power' will spend the rest of his days sitting in a cell for twenty-three hours a day. His visits and mail will be carefully monitored, decrypted if necessary, all of his visitors screened, and his visits recorded and analyzed. If he harbours any hope of pulling some secret strings, he will be very unhappy."

The General smiled at that thought.

"Besides, I had my fill of revenge that day, when I blew

up the back yard. Five of his agents died, I'm told." The look of remorse was evident in Mike's eyes.

"That's true..." Urnbreach answered, "...and their deaths have been re-classified. Initially, using some of his Washington connections, Reall muddied the waters. Their presence was made to look as if they were trying to stop "persons unknown" from completing the mission that they were on. The cover wasn't very convincing, but it was just good enough to raise a doubt. So, at first, they were classified as dying in the line of duty. Now that we know the truth, the record has been amended. Instead of 'In the line of duty', the file now reads 'During the commission of a capital crime.' Their names have been removed from the Role of Honour and further government benefits have been accordingly revoked."

"Max," Mike called, *"Please have the Dr. Michael Kelly Fund look into their family status and take appropriate action."* he requested.

"Sure thing, Mike; I'll take care of it," Max responded.

"Thanks, pal."

Mike and Gillian were married the following June. Father Don Fitzgerald, S.J. and Rabbi Philip Flickstein co-presided at their wedding. That might have meant the end of Mike's career as a trans-dimensional traveller, since Max confirmed definitively that he would be damaged if another neural interface was connected to his matrix alongside Mike's. While it was true that they could use the alternate AI at Twin Pines to send another man or woman on the next trip, with Gillian's blessing, Mike continued with Project Symphony.

www.ingramcontent.com/pod-product-compliance
Lightning Source LLC
Chambersburg PA
CBHW051453170626
46811CB00002B/461

* 9 7 8 0 9 9 4 0 6 3 9 0 8 *